Splinter Universe Presents!
The Wrong Lance

Sharon Lee and Steve Miller

Copyright Page

Splinter Universe Presents!
The Wrong Lance
Pinbeam Books: pinbeambooks.com

#

#

All of the content collected in this book has previously been posted to Splinter Universe (splinteruniverse.com).

#

Cover design by selfpubbookcovers.com/RLSather
ISBN: 978-1-948465-12-0

Thanks

to Mighty Tyop Hunters Chuck Diters and Deborah Fishburn
your efforts are appreciated!
Any typos or infelicities that remain in the text are the fault of the
authors

The Wrong Lance

Author's Introduction to
The Wrong Lance

As posted on Splinter Universe, May 25, 2020

Those of you who have been with us for a little while may recall that in early 2018, Steve and I threw away the first 70,000 words of a Liaden novel titled *Accepting the Lance*. It was not an easy decision—it's never an easy decision to throw out so many words—not even *bad* words, merely not the *right* words.

The way Steve and I work is that one of us is lead on each particular title—and we do swap off. The person who is lead on the project currently in hand has what is in essence a third vote, to be cast in case of a tie in case of a creative disagreement.

I was lead on *Lance,* and the . . . error is mine to own, the book died in my hands. I brought the cooling corpse to Steve and asked him to read it, in case it wasn't *really* dead, but only resting, because I had taken a minor wrong turn in direction. Sadly, his verdict was the same as mine: *It's dead, Jim.*

So, we did what we had to—we pitched those words, contacted Madame at Baen to report the death, and asked for a new delivery date, which she graciously provided.

And we started over. I was once again lead; I flatter myself that this time I got it right. *Accepting the Lance*, the Correct Edition, was published by Baen in December 2019.

Now, there's a Sekrit Thing that authors do—or rather, that we *don't* do—when a book dies and we "throw it out," and that is—we *don't delete* the wrong words. Good Ghod, no. Because—you never know. You never know when a scene in the wrong book will slot into the new book, and be Just The Thing.

Which is what happened with *Accepting the Lance*. Several scenes in *The Wrong Lance* will seem familiar to readers of the published novel. The scenes are included in the outtake because we wanted those reading along at home to have the Entire Experience of what it feels like when a narrative is rolling right along—and then drops in its tracks.

Now, I don't want to say too much in this introduction—I don't, let us say, want to spoil the experience of *The Wrong Lance* for you. I will say, however, that one of the reasons I identified later, which led to the story off-railing, is that I tried to continue the narrative directly from the last scene of *Neogenesis*. There's a tradition, see; people *expect* certain things from books written in series, such as direct sequels starting in certain places. I really felt pressured by this expectation, so I forced myself to start in the traditional way. This was, in retrospect, A Mistake.

Those who have read *Accepting the Lance* will note that I did not make that Mistake a second time. This allowed me to have access to pieces of the real story that I had turned my back on by starting in the Wrong Place.

. . . and I think that's enough to get us started. I hope that this exercise provides entertainment, and enlightenment. That's putting a lot on an outtake from a failed novel, but, really, the words are perfectly good, even if they're not canon.

To review, there are 11 chapters in *The Wrong Lance*, about 44,000 words. Chapter One will post next Monday, June 1, for Patrons Only on Patreon, and on Splinter Universe. For those coming in late, here's a link to the Things You Need to Know about this project.

'til next week, then – Sharon Lee.

Chapter One

Surebleak
Jelaza Kazone

Miri watched the car out of sight before turning back toward the house. She'd argued for the delm's office today, and Val Con hadn't fielded anything more than token resistance. Which meant they'd been on the same page, and it really didn't matter if that was courtesy of the lifemate link, or just a case of great minds thinking alike.

What mattered was getting him another set and order of problems to chew on, so he could come back fresh to the mess that was Clan Korval's on-going personal business. And, truth told, they *had* to open the Road Boss's office today—most especially with the survey team from TerraTrade still on-port, asking questions, counting heads, reviewing systems, and in general making everybody nervous.

There was, Miri acknowledged, as she walked down the hall to the delm's office, some risk in having Val Con on the same port as the survey team, but after the little dust-up at the reception, she counted on Team Leader Kasveini to make sure it was herself who conducted the interview with the Road Boss.

And, if it turned out that the team leader wasn't sensible, or wanted to push an issue, then she'd just have to depend on Val Con wanting Surebleak Port upgraded and certified more than he wanted to visit mayhem on idiots who questioned Korval's honor.

In the meantime, all they really had to do was to keep their heads down, and not do anything outlandish that skewed more attention their direction. How hard could that be?

She opened the door to the delm's office, and went directly to the buffet to pour herself a cup of coffee. The scanner was on, which was Val Con's habit. The names and home ports of ships incoming, and the filed destinations of ships outgoing imparted actual meaningful information to him. To her, not having been raised to have a familiarity of ships and ports and politics, the scanner was at best an occasional amusement and at worst just . . . noise.

Still, she didn't detour on the way to the desk to turn the thing off. Today, the calm voices talking over the details of her homeworld's traffic were . . . comforting.

She pulled the chair out, checked to be sure a cat hadn't taken possession before her, and sat down, tapping the screen on.

There was mail in the delm's in-box. Not exactly a surprise.

She pulled up the first, which was from Ms. dea'Gauss, acknowledging receipt of the delm's direction to discover funding for the clan's newly acquired space station. She assured them that the project was a priority, and that she expected to have preliminary figures within the week. In the meanwhile, she allowed that a schematic of the station, systems inventory, a list of needed upgrades in order of urgency, as well as a detailed report on the damaged portion of the ring, would assist her greatly in her work. Also, if the station keepers would send their estimate of expected traffic and a ranked list of services and amenities required by said traffic, that, too, would be of assistance.

Miri sipped coffee while she wondered whether the keepers had any notion how much traffic they were likely to see, and what services the Free Ships she understood were expected to be Tinsori Light's main clientele would want most. Well, they had Tolly Jones to consult, there.

She shook her head.

"Gonna be a job of work," she commented to no one in particular. And that was *before* anybody figured out how Free Ships paid their bills.

"Jeeves—" she began—

"Sleet and snow!" the scanner shouted. "Didja see that! It come right outta the sun, I'm tellin' you! No signature, no glare—"

"Meteor alert! Incoming! Keep to assigned orbits. If you are on approach, stay on course."

Miri spun to stare at the scanner. Meteor? She thought. Came right out of the sun, was it? She felt a slight chill in the warm office.

"Jeeves, can you see that rock?"

"Yes, Miri. I am coordinating with *Bechimo*. The route is unconventional, but we believe that it is a *route*, nor is the object detritus—"

"A ship," she interrupted, realizing that she had come to her feet.

"Yes," Jeeves said again. "I have a broad match with the Clutch vessel that transported Korval's holdings to Surebleak. However, the vessel incoming is much smaller, and—ah. *Bechimo* has backtracked to the entry point. We have very good reason to believe that it is using the electron substitution drive. I have extrapolated its course—on a heading for—"

"Our back field?"

"No, Miri. It is on course for our driveway."

She blinked.

"Odds of survival?"

"One hundred percent," Jeeves said promptly. "It is already slowing its descent. I estimate arrival in—"

"I have a communication from the approaching vessel," came a pleasant, unfamiliar voice. Comm Officer Joyita that must be, Miri thought, patching in on the shielded house line. She decided to be pissed about that later.

"Proceed, please, Mister Joyita," she said.

"Yes, ma'am. Pilot identifies herself as Emissary Twelve and states she is on the business of the Elders. An immediate meeting with the Delm of Korval is requested." There was a small pause.

"She apologizes for this unseemly haste, and pleads . . . necessity, ma'am."

"Thank you, Mister Joyita." Miri sighed, and turned toward the door.

"Jeeves, with me, please."

"Yes, Miri."

"Readiness report," she said, walking quickly, but not running, toward the front door.

"The nursery has been sealed and shielded. House shields are engaged. The Southern Suite has been sealed, by agreement with Captain Waitley. I am recording, and sending live to the office of the Road Boss."

"Does Mister Joyita have permission to access in-house communications?"

"Miri, he does, retroactively. We had been discussing comm security protocols, as he had been kind enough to point out an error in my configurations. This present event overtook us before I could effect a repair."

"I see."

She felt a slight niggle at the back of her mind, and glimpsed a glitter of intense and tightly-woven pattern. Val Con had the feed, now, and was focused on it, all his training to the fore. He wasn't worried, so far as she could tell, and that soothed her in a way Jeeves' assurances hadn't.

Still, she thought, coming to a branching of the hall; big rocks that were only small in comparison to out-of-reason enormous rocks, coming down 'way too close to a good subsection of the people she cared about most. Even the Clutch made mistakes—at least, she assumed so.

And, if the house shields were up, there wasn't one damn' bit of good in her going to the door.

She turned right and followed the hall to the morning parlor, where there was a screen. For that matter, there was a screen in the delm's office, but she hadn't been thinking, had she?

It was then that she felt it, a warm pressure, as if he had kissed her cheek.

Smiling, she stepped into the parlor.

"Show me, please," she said.

The screen came live, one half displaying the projected course, with deceleration rates, approach path, and approximate time of arrival on their doorstep.

The other half of the screen showed the object itself, rock-like as it was. As she watched, a ghost overlaid the approaching vessel—the image of the ship that had brought Jelaza Kazone, house and Tree, all of yos'Galan's household goods, with room left over for a few atmosphere fliers to get tucked 'round the edges—to Surebleak.

"Courier ship," she said. Jeeves must've figured she was talking to herself, because he didn't answer.

She felt the sense of Val Con's interested attention intensify, and then fade, as if he was satisfied with both the ship and its proposed docking; and had stepped back into being Road Boss.

Frowning, she scrutinized the screens again. Half an hour, more or less, before Emissary Twelve was with them. Time for a cup of coffee.

She'd just drawn a mugful from the carafe on the buffet when she heard the clatter of boots on the front stair. With a nod, she picked up another mug and filled it from the tea pot.

Light steps moved down the hall, and she turned, mug in hand, offering an easy smile.

"Hey, Theo. Want some tea?"

Val Con's sister blinked, and shook her wispy pale hair back from her face. She had the family features—pointed chin, decisive nose, well-marked brows—but her expressions were more open than were usually found among her kin, even when they were being deliberately broad, for the benefit of children and Terrans.

"Tea'd be great, thanks," Theo said, coming forward to take the mug.

"*Bechimo* says there's a Clutch ship coming in for a landing."

"Jeeves says the same. If we're to believe the message caught by Mister Joyita, we're expecting Emissary Twelve, who needs to see the delm immediately, and who's sorry for the bother, but pleads necessity."

Theo paused with the mug half-way to her mouth.

"*Necessity?*" she repeated.

"That's the message."

"When—" Theo began, then stopped, her gaze jumping to the screens.

"I saw—*Bechimo* showed me the route in. They'll be lucky if they're only slapped with a fine."

Miri blinked.

"Gods, I hadn't even thought of that. As soon's the portmaster realizes it's a ship, not a rock, she's going to have to fine 'em. Especially with the—"

BOOM.

* * *

Tapout Quarry

"How many are viable?" the driver asked, pulling the all-terrain buggy close to the edge of the quarry lip.

The passenger brushed her fingers over her screen in an arcane pattern, looked up, her face pinched with cold.

"Of the six in the pit, three. They will do little for us beyond adding to the noise. The four over there—"

She used her chin to point at the field beyond, where machinery hulked, rust-colored and quiescent in the dim light.

"Those four are walkers; equipped with blades, scythes, grinders, and other instruments of destruction. All four are viable, and ought to remain so for a significant time."

The driver consulted the on-board map, then squinted out over the land, gauging direction.

"More than a diversion," he said at last, and with satisfaction.

"Oh, indeed; food-crops cannot hope to stand against those," the passenger said. She paused as if considering the question fairly. "Nor could a farmer."

"Once they're started, they'll go until they meet with an accident, or run out of fuel?"

"They will continue unless or until they meet with an accident," the passenger said. "They are self-powered. The longer they walk, the more fuel they have available to them."

"What're the chances of them having a set o'keys?"

"Slim. Management would have kept the keys and the codes. If either had been available to those left behind, the machines would surely have been put to work, rather than left to rust."

"Good," said the driver. "Fire at will."

The passenger tapped her screen in a rapid sequence.

Across the quarry, one of the large pieces of equipment shifted. Lights came on at the apex, as if some giant creature had opened its eyes. It rolled forward slightly, gears clashing and snarling. The racket seemed to wake its comrades; lights snapped on, great blades flexed, and they began—slowly at first, but rapidly picking up speed—to move, down the hill and toward the village at its base.

* * *

Dudley Avenue and Farley Lane

It might have been a roll of thunder that waked Daav. If so, it waked *only* him. His bedmates slumbered on, Kamele's head on Aelliana's shoulder; a pleasant picture, which he tarried a moment to admire before slipping out from beneath the blankets.

His pants came easily to hand, and he pulled them on before turning toward the window. A line of very bright light showed at the edge of the drawn shade; he eased it up a fraction and gazed upon a morning already well underway, and a brilliant, cloudless sky. Well, then, possibly it had only thundered in his dreams. Certainly, it would not have been the first time.

He let the shade fall back, looking again to the bed, and the pair slumbering there. Given the advancing hour, he really ought to wake them. Surely they had tried Kareen's patience—and her hospitality—far enough. He and Aelliana had stopped for a morning visit, and had proceeded to monopolize Kamele all day. They ought, he told himself wryly, to have expected that—after so much time, and so many adventures, in which Aelliana's physical presence, and his own abrupt youthening, were not the least strange—of course it would take hours—days!—to catch themselves up. It had been his error, to expect that Kamele would meet them coldly. His *grievous* error, unworthy of the man who had been Kamele Waitley's *onagrata* for twenty Standards.

Well, and he had his error shown to him, and they three had filled in the broad outlines, at least. His sister had been forbearing, and perhaps even kind—witness the discreet series of trays sent up to the scholar's office, and the lack of a call to Prime.

To tell truth, neither he nor Aelliana had planned a bed visit, nor, he was persuaded, had Kamele. Yet, when the moment came, it had been recognized by all, and accepted as inevitable.

So—a touch, and another, a press, a stroke; knowing kisses shared between familiar lovers—and the bed, all three aflame. And after they had rested, once again, comfortable and comforting, before sliding into shared sleep . . .

To wake and find morning busy before them.

As if to punctuate that thought, there came a discreet knock at the door, which was very likely their eviction notice.

Running his hands over his short-cropped hair, he crossed the room and opened the door, expecting to see his sister, frowning her irritation. Instead, there was another tray on the table beside the door, a multitude of small covered plates clustered on it, with a steaming teapot, and a carafe of morning wine nestled next to a small vase holding three small dark red flowers.

Well.

He picked up the tray, brought it into the room, and put it on the table by the window.

Daav, Aelliana murmured inside his head; *has Kareen had enough of us?*

Very much the contrary, he told her. *True affection is honored, and we are invited to make merry.*

We HAVE made merry, Aelliana pointed out.

Ah, but have we been merry thrice? He asked, focusing deliberately on the vase and its contents.

There was a flicker of *something* from Aelliana. Perhaps it was astonishment.

KAREEN sent that?

So I suppose, as it was Kareen who urged us to call and make our bows. She must feel a certain proprietary interest. And she does appear genuinely fond of Kamele.

She is . . . much changed, Aelliana offered eventually.

I am told that age mellows, he answered. *Not that I would know, of course.*

Of course, his lifemate said politely. *If you have done fussing with the tray, you might come and help me wake Kamele.*

Daav smiled, and bowed gently to the three bold flowers in their vase.

Certainly, he said. *After all, one would scarcely wish to disoblige one's sister.*

#

Later, having obliged Kareen most thoroughly, they tardily addressed breakfast, each telling over the tasks of the advancing day.

"We have two ships to inspect, so that we may vigorously debate the merits of each," Aelliana said, sipping the last of her tea.

Kamele tipped her head to one side. Her hair was still damp from the shower, and droplets glittered like gemstones, strung through her pale curls.

"Will you set up as small traders?" she asked.

"As couriers," Aelliana said. "We are quite unsuited to be traders, I fear."

"And it must be said," Daav added, "that the potential of randomized danger draws her, like a moth to flame."

"Very true," Aelliana said gravely. "Besides, you know, if I fail to fall into enough scrapes from which I must be extracted, Daav becomes bored, which I am certain you agree is to be avoided."

Kamele laughed.

"When he's bored, he takes things apart," she said, giving Aelliana a comradely nod; "as you know. You'd definitely want to avoid that, on a spaceship."

"Unkind!" Daav protested; "I always put them back together again!"

He put his empty cup on the table, and met Kamele's eye, lifting a shoulder in a half-shrug. "Nearly always."

She laughed again.

"Do you plan an immediate lift?"

"Not quite immediately," Aelliana said. "The debating of merits may take some time. Also, we must be tested for new licenses."

Kamele frowned, and glanced to Daav.

"Theo tells me that a master pilot's license never expires."

"Very true, but in the particular case, it is—*more expedient,* let us say—to obtain a new license under a new name than to undertake an explanation of my current estate to either the Pilots Guild or to the Scouts."

"The delm is adamant," Aelliana added. "We must qualify on our current abilities, and the tickets we fly on must be true."

"No falsifying sources," Kamele said wisely, and was rewarded with a wide smile.

"Exactly so."

"And you?" Daav said. "Are you entirely fixed on resigning your position at Delgado?"

"Yes. I'll be sending my letter this week. I expect Admin will be delighted. I've been more of a thorn in their side than a rose in their crown, lately."

"I wonder . . ." Aelliana said, and hesitated, casting Kamele a conscious look. "I fear that I am about to meddle."

Kamele met her eyes blandly.

"Well, I'm certainly not used to that."

Aelliana inclined her head gravely.

"Indeed, how could you be? Now that you have been warned, I proceed—Kamele, *must* you resign?"

"What else should I do? Go back to Delgado and be compliant?"

"Oh, no; that would be too dreadful! I was only thinking that—*of course,* you will wish to use your expertise to build Surebleak an educational system. Surebleak, though, is short of funds, and likewise short of scholars trained in the traditional way. How if you allowed Delgado to participate in the project? Would not a satellite school on a planet which is poised to enter the universal conversation increase Admin's *melant'i*, and the whole worth of the university?"

"Especially," Daav murmured; "if they could assign some of their more . . . non-compliant scholars to the project?"

Kamele stared . . . toward him, though she was seeing her thoughts. It was an expression he knew well.

Our work here is done, van'chela, he said to Aelliana.

We may trust so. And only think what a gaggle of Delgadan scholars might do with Surebleak.

Imagination balks, he assured her.

Bah.

Kamele blinked back to the room.

"I take your point," she said to Aelliana. "This is an op—"

She was interrupted by sudden commotion in the hallway, followed by a pounding on her door.

Daav came to his feet, and moved across the room. Behind him, Aelliana rose to stand between Kamele and the door, one hand in her pocket.

He spared a thought for his own hideaway, then simply jerked the door violently open.

Amiz, Kareen's personal bodyguard, stood framed in the doorway, both hands in plain sight.

"Sorry to interrupt," he said quickly, "but there's Mister Jeeves on-comm calling for Professor Waitley's guests to go up to the Road Boss's house, quick! He says there's *Clutch involved*."

He hesitated, and eyed Daav speculatively.

"He said you'd know what that meant."

Clutch? Daav thought.

How fortunate that we are at home, Aelliana commented dryly.

Daav did not laugh. Instead he nodded to Amiz.

"Indeed; we know precisely what it means," he said, stretching the truth in the interest of preserving calm and order.

"Thank you. Please tell Jeeves that we are on our way."

Chapter Two

Surebleak
The Bedel

The sound bellowed across the camp, echoing in the garden, rattling the steam pipes inside their confining metal belts, intruding, even, into the din and thunder of Rafin's forge.

The *kompani* leapt to their feet as one, hearts pounding, breath caught. Not one among them had ever heard that alarm, yet all knew it for what it was.

Droi had been sitting beside her hearth, having just finished her first cup of tea. Kezzi, who had been sharing her tent in accordance with the *luthia's* wisdom, had just gotten to her feet, and Malda with her. Kezzi was to go up into the City Above, and the *gadje* school, while the dog stayed with Droi and Maysl, her child within.

She froze, looking down at Droi, dark eyes wide.

"The ship!" she said.

"No," Droi said, forcibly calm, and as if the distinction made the moment less significant. "Only *news* of the ship."

She put the mug on the hearth stone, and struggled to get her feet fairly under her. Her belly defeated this effort, as had become its habit. Droi sighed, and held up her hands.

"Help me rise," she said moderately, though it was hard for her to ask for aid.

Kezzi obeyed with alacrity, and in addition made certain to stand so that a steadying shoulder was within reach, should Droi's feet be momentarily foolish.

In this moment, she was steady enough, though her blood remained chilled by the klaxon's blare. It was quiet now, having destroyed the *kompani's* peace, and already there were those of her brothers and sisters moving past her hearth on the way to the common fire.

To hear news of the ship.

"I'll be late for school," Kezzi said, keeping pace as Droi turned her face, as well, toward the gather-place.

School had become important to Kezzi, as had her brother in the City Above. It had come to Droi just lately, as she dozed and dreamed by her hearth, communing with Maysl—it had come to her that the *kompani* had developed many ties with the *gadje* here, on this world. There was Kezzi and her brother; Silain the *luthia* with the Lady and the Professor; Udari, Memit, Syaera, and Isart with the madman at the end of the road; Rys and his Brother Undertree, not to mention his mad oath to the Headwoman there . . .

Indeed, thought Droi, it had come to her a few nights ago that the common thread running through all these now-woven relationships—was Rys. Rys, who was himself an outsider, until he had stood before the fire and bound himself, soul and heart, to the *kompani*, accepting the Bedel as his brothers and sisters. Rys had also bound himself in brotherhood to Val Con yos'Phelium, Headman of the People of the Tree; Kezzi's brother Syl Vor was of that folk, as were Lady Kareen and Professor Waitley.

The madman, Farmer Yulie Shaper, might as well be undertree, as near as his holding stood, and it had been Rys' brother the headman who had brought news of the work to Memit, who had brought it to Silain the *luthia*, who had dreamed upon it . . .

. . . and now there were four gone from the *kompani* to the far end of the Port Road, to help Yulie Shaper take in his crops.

"Droi?" Kezzi said again. "I'll be late for school. Syl Vor will worry, if I don't send a message."

The brother, yes. Yes, he *would* worry, being, by everything Droi had heard, a tender boy, who would, she made no doubt, grow into a man of heart.

"We must to the fire," Droi said. "Your brother's mother is a *luthia*, is she not?"

Kezzi nodded.

"So. She will advise him. This thing—is of the *kompani* . . ."

She shivered suddenly, black showing ragged at the edge of her vision.

"This," she said, feeling the burn in her blood, "will *alter the fate* of the *kompani*. We must all of us be present, to witness."

Her foot caught on an uneven stone, and she staggered. Kezzi thrust a shoulder beneath her questing hand, and, so steadied, they went on, in silence.

After all, Droi thought, Kezzi was Silain the *luthia's* 'prentice. She knew a foretelling when she heard one.

The common fire was lit, the Bedel grouped in a half-circle facing it. A hand rose in the air, which was Luma, Maysl's hearth-mother, beckoning them.

They joined her, Kezzi and Luma helping Droi to the blanket, before sitting, one to a side, and Malda curled on Kezzi's lap. They gave their attention to the fire, before which stood Alosha the headman, Silain the *luthia*, and Pulka, who listened along the byways of the stars.

The Bedel, so say the Bedel of themselves, speak with many voices, as heedless of their song as the birds. Yet, it was not so, this day. Those assembled sat quiet, tension roiling above their silence.

Up before the gather-fire, she saw Silain the *luthia* make a small gesture, and the air lightened somewhat. Droi drew an easier breath, sighed it out, and put her hand on her belly.

Maysl, she said inside her head, *attend this well.*

She felt her daughter's attention sharpen, even as Alosha the headman took one step forward, and raised his hands.

"All of you heard the klaxon," Alosha said. "We have received a message from the ship. Pulka will explain the nature of that message, and what is required of the *kompani*."

He stepped back to Silain's side; Pulka took one step forward.

He looked, Droi thought, tired, and very nearly grim. Pulka was not, by nature, a happy man, nor was he a stern one. A placid man, who liked his comforts; who could, occasionally, be nagged into brilliance. Very little in life was sharp enough to cut Pulka. The ship's message though, which he would have been the first to read, had burned a tiny scar on his heart. Looking with *luthia's* eyes, Droi could see it, still hot and hurtful.

"Sisters and brothers," Pulka said; "we have this morning received a message from the ship. It is not a direct message, meant for this *kompani* alone, but an automated dispatch, which has been wide-cast to several *kompanis* such as ours, which have missed their pick-up date by a certain number of years."

He paused, in anticipation, Droi knew, of the flood of questions which would normally engulf him at this point.

There was silence; not one voice was raised, no single one of the *kompani* rose to their feet to speak.

Pulka cleared his throat; glancing at Alosha the headman, who gave him a grave nod, and turned again to face those waiting, silent, and finished what he had to say.

"The ship requires an answer. If we fail to answer, it will assume that we have not heard; that we are, in fact, Lost, and the logs will reflect this as our *kompani's* fate. The ship will not query again."

Another pause, but the exclamations of horror, of outrage did not arise.

"A proper answer to the ship requires codes which I have dreamed. When that answer is returned, the ship will flag it for the captain, who will review it; and who will eventually send pick-up instructions and an estimated time of the ship's arrival."

At long last, one of the *kompani* raised herself to her feet, Jin, the *luthia's* good right hand.

"How long," she asked, "will it be, after a message is sent, for the ship to arrive here for us?"

Pulka showed empty palms.

"That, we cannot know. Such information will doubtless be given us, when the captain responds to our ack."

"Thank you, brother."

Jin sat down. Pulka waited for more questions.

Droi, sitting beside Kezzi and Luma, had many questions, though none that she would willingly shout out before all the *kompani*. She—the ship was so late, she had thought it would never come; that it had forgotten them. And yet, here was news; the ship had not forgotten; it remembered. And that—that altered *everything*.

From the far edge of the circle rose a tall, powerful figure—Rafin.

"Why did the ship not come," he asked, "at the appointed time?"

Again, Pulka showed empty hands.

"That, too, we will doubtless be told, later. This automatic sending; it only seeks acknowledgment; it does not give reasons."

"We are certain, then, that this is from the ship. *Our ship?*" Rafin pursued, which was, Droi thought, a good question, and one which had not been among the dozen others clamoring inside her head.

"I have confirmed that it is from the ship. It is on the correct band; it utilizes the correct codes; it matches all the necessary protocols. If you want to do so, come to me, and I will show you the message itself."

"I will do that, brother," said Rafin, and sat down again.

Pulka looked 'round.

"If any others are interested, come to me and I will show you the protocols, the bands, the codes, the match-ups. I have, also, the original dream from the communications technician who was set down with the *kompani*, if any wish to dream it."

There was a small murmur 'round the circle at that, and here came another of the *kompani* to his feet. Apparently, thought Droi, her brothers and sisters were beginning to waken from their shock.

"How long," asked that brother, and Pulka blinked.

"I—" he began.

"No, I'll ask it proper," said the brother. "How long do we have to dream on this? Before the ship needs its answer?"

And that, thought Droi, was the most interesting question at all. In story, in dreams, every *kompani* is eager to be taken up again into the bosom of the ship. It would seem that her brothers and sisters had not embraced these stories with all their hearts.

Alosha the headman stepped forward; Pulka dropped back one step, to stand next to the *luthia*.

"The ship needs its reply at once," said Alosha. "There are technical reasons for this that Pulka is also able to explain. But, there is no call for a decision on this matter. The decision was made when this *kompani* was formed. We guaranteed to return to the ship with those things we had learned, and those things which we had found. That the ship is late makes no difference to our guarantee."

He paused and looked around the circle, his gaze seeming to rest on each one of them in turn.

"We have heard the ship," said Alosha the headman; "and we will answer the ship. We are here; we are ready for pick-up."

Chapter Three

Surebleak
Jelaza Kazone

It sat, steaming gently, on the driveway, not much bigger, Miri thought, than the forty-eight-seat touring bus mothballed in the garage. There was no visible hatch, no visible instrumentation, or lights. No obvious identification.

Just a rock, that was all.

"Good landing," Theo noted from beside her. "Didn't even dimple the tarmac."

That was a point in its favor, Miri allowed, but not enough to off-set her growing irritation.

She turned her head to address the man-high canister topped by a ball that was at the moment glowing palely orange.

"Jeeves, please ask Mr. Joyita to find out when our visitor intends to emerge. The delm of Korval awaits. Impatiently."

"Transmitting the delm's request," Jeeves said agreeably.

There was a brief pause, followed by Joyita's voice.

"The pilot thanks the delm of Korval for the gift of her time. She will emerge with all haste."

A crack appeared in the rock's pitted surface, and another. Soundlessly a hatch opened, and a figure, stooped, yet still taller than either Miri or Theo, emerged, moving awkwardly.

It achieved the surface of the drive and straightened—a very young Clutch, Miri saw, the shell no bigger than a field pack high up on the back. Pockets and bags depended from a vest woven from what seemed to be leather strips.

"I am called for the purpose of this mission, Emissary Twelve." The voice was light; nowhere near Edger's occasionally head-rattling boom. "I am charged by the Elders to deliver a message to the delm of Korval."

Miri took a breath—and Val Con was there. She felt the full presence of him, like he was standing at her shoulder, regarding the Emissary gravely.

"We are," she said, in High Liaden, surprising herself, at least. "*We are* the delm of Korval. Our kinswoman and house security attend us. They may hear the words of the Elders, which we stand ready to receive."

"I am to approach the delm of Korval in all their names and faces, and inform them that the Elders have been aware of a flaw in the fabric of the universe. They have accorded it long study as they sought to understand its nature and to formulate an appropriate response."

Emissary Twelve paused to blink enormous eyes.

"The flaw has vanished; the fabric of the universe is healed."

Well, thought Miri, it was nice to have corroboration, though she wouldn't have predicted receiving it from this particular source. Clutch lived a really long time. That given, they didn't tend to be quick to notice change.

"The state and energies of the universe are now what they were within the memory of the eldest of the Elders, who had scarcely been hatched when the anomaly occurred," Emissary Twelve continued. She tipped her head slightly, maybe approximating a bow.

"The Elders ask if the delm of Korval and the Elder Tree which the delm serves is aware of this circumstance."

"Yes," Miri said, in unison with Val Con; "we are aware."

There was a pause, not really that long, considering the source.

"If the answer to this query was in the affirmative, I was to ask further. Did the delm of Korval or the Elder Tree effect this healing?"

"The Tree assisted a clan member in the action," Val Con said by himself while Miri was trying to figure out where this was going. If the Clutch Elders had been aware of the tear, wound, whatever, in the fabric of the universe—well, it couldn't be a *bad thing* to save the universe . . .

Could it?

"The answers given are within tolerances," Emissary Twelve stated. "The Elders would have the destroyer of the universe brought to them, so that an examination may go forth."

OK, that *definitely* didn't sound good.

Val Con bowed slightly, which meant she did, too. Beside them, Theo wasn't saying anything at all, smart girl, standing alert and poised.

"I regret that the clan member responsible for preserving the universe that the Elders cohabit with the delm of Korval, the Tree, and countless other intelligences, is from home," Val Con said tartly. "He and his lifemate were gravely injured, and there is some question whether either will fully recover what they have lost. They have placed themselves into the hands of the Healers, from whose care we will remove them for no reason less than the imminent extinction of another universe."

"You should also know," Miri said, keeping to High Liaden; "that he does not remember what happened. The details were already fading when he returned to us, after the mission was done."

Eyes the size of soup tureens gazed at her mournfully.

"I apologize for my haste, which has caused you distress. The Elders have given me no instruction in the event of an imperfect memory."

"Even if that were not so," Val Con said in a tone that brooked no argument, "it is not for the Elders to decide for one of Korval. *Korval* decides for Korval, and our judgment is this: our wounded child will remain here, where he is shielded and safe, until he has recovered so far as he might."

Silence.

Blink.

"Yes," said Emissary Twelve. "I ask if the Elder Tree recalls the event and the actions."

Miri felt a flutter of green at the edge of her awareness. The Tree was paying attention, too. The Tree, she thought, might even be *interested*. That was unsettling.

"The Tree recalls the event with some amount of pride," Val Con said. "It is willing to speak with you, and impart the particulars, so that you may carry its account to the Elders."

Impossibly, Emissary Twelve's big eyes got bigger.

"I! I am the emissary sent by the Elders. It is to the Elders the Tree must speak."

"That's gonna be tricky," Miri said, in Terran.

Emissary Twelve closed her eyes.

Miri sighed.

"Look," she said; "Maybe the Elders can send somebody at a higher pay grade to take the Tree's testimony and maybe talk to our clan member, when he's in better shape," she said. "Twelfth Shell Fifth Hatched Knife Clan of Middle River's Spring Spawn of Farmer Greentrees of the Spearmaker's Den: The Edger might be a good choice. If he's not available, then I'd suggest Seventh Shell Third Hatched Knife Clan of Middle River's Spring Spawn of Farmer Greentrees of the Spearmaker's Den: The Sheather."

Emissary Twelve opened her eyes.

"That is for the Elders to say. I have been provided with an option which may be adapted to this case. In the event that the Destroyer of Universes had died of his efforts, I was to bring Daav yos'Phelium to the Elders."

"Daav yos'Phelium," Val Con said carefully, "was not involved in the effort to preserve our universe."

"Daav yos'Phelium gave his word to the Elders that he would answer their further questions, should any arise. Further questions have arisen."

"That is unfortunate," Val Con said. "Daav yos'Phelium has, in the time since the Elders received his word, died."

Well, thought Miri, that *was* true, so far as it went. It was damn' near an art form among Liadens, to see how close they could shave to the exact truth, and still mislead. As true-lies went, in fact, this one was almost unsubtle, but apparently Val Con was so determined to keep kin close he was willing to sacrifice style points.

Emissary Twelve was silent. Her chest was seen to rise—and fall.

"Surely Daav yos'Phelium would have left his unfulfilled promises in the care of a second," she said. "I believe this is a Liaden custom."

Score one for Emissary Twelve, Miri thought, even as she felt the sting of Val Con's irritation.

"Jeeves," she said; "would you please ask Kor Vid yos'Phelium and his partner to join us? Tell him the Clutch would like to speak with him."

"Relaying message. He is at Lady Kareen's house; it may be some time before he arrives."

"Understood." Miri looked to Emissary Twelve.

The kid was exhausted, she thought, and who wouldn't be? She had to've strung a dozen Jumps or more together to get here so soon after Ren Zel's little act of heroism. And now that she was arrived, the delm of Korval wasn't sticking to the script.

"The house offers hospitality," Val Con said, in her voice; "refreshment, and a quiet place to recover from your exertions until the pilots arrive."

"The offer does the house honor," Emissary Twelve said, and you'd've said she was squaring her shoulders, if she'd had shoulders in the proper way. "The order from the Elders was *with all haste*. Therefore, I will now speak with the Elder Tree."

"Sure," said Miri. "I'll show you the way."

She turned to Theo, who was looking like she was going to bite the kid's head off, and maybe Miri's, too.

"You wanna bring the pilots to the Tree if we're not back by the time they get here?"

Give her credit, Theo's face didn't get any *more* sour.

"Yes," she said.

"Thanks." Miri stepped forward, feeling Val Con at her side, and beckoned to Emissary Twelve. "Right this way. With me, Jeeves—Oh, and Jeeves?"

"Yes, Miri?"

"You can bring house systems to normal, when you get time."

"Yes, Miri."

* * *

Theo watched as Miri and Jeeves—or maybe it was Miri, *Val Con*, and Jeeves—guided Emissary Twelve down the drive, toward the garden gate.

"Theo? What troubles you?" *Bechimo's* voice was inside her head, in the place she thought of as *bond-space*; where she and *Bechimo* shared math and piloting approaches; where she was able to see ship's systems as *Bechimo* did, and the coruscating fabrics of space.

"Val Con," she said quietly. "He was *here*. With Miri. *Sharing* Miri."

"Joyita's research indicates that such abilities may often be found among what the literature signifies as *true lifematings*, or *wizard's matches*."

Theo blinked.

"Why is Joyita researching lifemates?" she asked, but she had a feeling that she already knew the answer to that question.

"When your brother Val Con was on this vessel, seeking information on which to build his field judgment, he asked if we—you and I—were lifemated. I of course said that we were not."

Her brother Val Con had been a scout, and their shared parent had been a scout. She'd always considered it part of Father's personality—part of what made him *Father*—that he asked so many questions—and none of them idle.

Possibly, she thought now, it was a scout thing—something they had been trained in, like Father's specialty in Cultural Genetics.

Or maybe only particularly nosy people became scouts.

"Theo?"

"So, why is Joyita researching this and not you?"

"I am not researching the question, because I *know* the answer," *Bechimo* answered, bad-temperedly. "You and I—the captain and the ship—*are bonded*, as the Builders intended, in order to make a more perfect partnership which protects and sustains the crew and the route; the captain and the ship.

"Joyita, however, has decided to indulge in mischief."

That was a little sharp, Theo thought—and also unfair.

"But maybe it's not mischief. My brother asked me the same question—and I told him the same thing you did, that we're bonded. But, that—"

She waved in the direction that the Clutch had been escorted.

"We already knew that Miri and Val Con each know where the other is—*can feel* where the other one is—even when they're out of sight. And we just saw him . . . *join her* to talk to Emissary Twelve, even though he's at the Port office.

"Val Con's really alert to details, patterns—and he makes connections. When you and I talk in bond-space, it must *look enough* like what he and Miri do that he—made the match. It's an interesting connection; I can see why Joyita's intrigued. Please ask him to keep me informed on the progress of his research."

There was silence in bond-space. Maybe even petulant silence. Before Theo could decide, she heard the sound of a door opening behind her. She turned around as Kara stepped out of the house, Hevelin perched on her shoulder.

"Trouble?"

Kara made a wry face.

"Insistence. Ambassador Hevelin has a *great need* to visit with the Elder Tree and also to associate with the pilot who just arrived in that—" she used her chin to the point at the boulder in the driveway—"to find whom she knows."

She sighed, and showed Theo empty hands palm-up, and the suggestion of a shrug.

"Once the shields were dropped, it was far easier to bring him, than to argue."

Theo shifted her attention to the oh-so-innocent norbear on Kara's shoulder, and frowned, hard.

"You're getting to be a nuisance," she told him. "*And* a bully."

She caught a flutter of distress; Hevelin was sorry she was upset, and his good friend Kara, too.

The distress morphed into something harder; Theo glimpsed a sort of glittery grey rock, and raised her eyebrows.

"But?" she prompted.

"Ah," said Kara; "this approach is familiar. He is about to plead his *melant'i*."

Indeed, a series of images flowed to Theo: Hevelin curled against a plump white norbear with a black spot before each ear. Hevelin conversing with a rangy woman with knowing eyes and short-cropped brown hair. Hevelin sitting on Clarence's lap, surveying the board. Hevelin meeting Grakow. Hevelin disciplining Stost. Hevelin holding a gun, safety off, nose pointed toward the decking.

Theo blinked, and murmured for Kara's benefit: "I'm getting Sinaya and Guild Master Constance from Velaskiz Rotundo; Clarence maybe running through board drills; Stost getting yelled at; Grakow; and his, um, quick reactions to the loose gun on Minot Station."

She glanced at Kara.

"Is that the sequence you got?"

"Very exactly."

"Well, it's persuasive," Theo said; "but what're we supposed to be persuaded *of*?"

"I believe the narrative has to do with Hevelin's obligations and accomplishments as an ambassador for his race, and an operative for the Pilot's Guild. It is, one understands, nothing less than his duty to expand the net of his acquaintance."

"He's got a point, there," Theo said. "That's what the Guild set him up to do."

"I do not dispute it. It is the contention that his point carries all others before it that I question."

"Well, it can't." Theo considered the norbear, receiving once more the impression of stone. "Emissary Twelve, who just landed, has urgent business with the Tree, and with a pilot who's been called to the house to deal with her. Your business has to wait on hers, and it might be that she doesn't have any time for you. She seemed kind of rushed, and under a lot of pressure. You've got to expect that, sometimes at least, somebody else's duty takes precedence."

Hevelin granted her argument, graciously, and repeated his necessity, with the assurance that he would be very quick, and seek only a few key connections, to establish a point from which to dream further.

"That is very handsome of you," Kara said, having apparently caught that bit fair. "However, Theo's case stands; no matter your necessity, it is possible that you will not be permitted to speak with Emissary Twelve. In this case, her duties carry more weight than yours."

Hevelin begged leave to doubt this.

Kara tapped her foot, and looked to Theo.

"Permission to tutor Ambassador Hevelin on the workings of *melant'i*, especially with regard to relative necessity."

Theo stared at her.

"*Relative* necessity?" she repeated. "I thought necessity was absolute."

"In many applications, it may seem so," Kara said. "However, given two necessities—the example my grandmother relished was—the necessity to put out a fire in the garage before it reaches the flammables, and the necessity to arrive at a formal dinner on time—the necessity which produces the more immediate consequences has precedence."

She gave Theo a droll look.

"The necessity of not blowing up the garage, the house, and the neighborhood clearly bears the greatest weight in the example, even should an important alliance be strained or lost by a tardy arrival at the table."

"Maybe you ought to tutor me, too," Theo said, ruefully.

"It will be my pleasure to mark out the pertinent paragraphs in the Code for you to sleep-learn, and to discuss them with you, after."

"I have the references in the *Liaden Code of Proper Conduct*, Theo," *Bechimo* said in bond-space. "They are tagged and you may refer to them at need."

"Thank you," Theo answered. "Talking the nuances over with Kara will help me really know the material, rather than having it on file."

"As you will." *Bechimo* said shortly—and withdrew.

Theo blinked back to the driveway in time to see Kara frowning at her.

"*Bechimo* was letting me know that he had marked out the passages for me and put them in a reference file," Theo explained.

"Ah," Kara answered, her voice absolutely even. "And you said?"

"I said that your plan—sleep-learning bolstered by discussion—would insure that I'd really *learn* the material, rather than needing to look it up every time there was need."

"Just so," Kara said.

It seemed like she was about to say something else—then decided against. She turned away, Hevelin on her shoulder, and walked over to the boulder-ship sitting on the driveway, its hatch still up.

It had, Theo saw, stopped steaming, but that didn't necessarily mean it was cool.

"This is a very strange vessel," Kara said. "A rock? Where is the drive? Where are the coils?"

She took another step closer, and Theo moved toward her, ready to snatch her back, if anything untoward happened.

Nothing did happen, though, other than Kara pausing at a respectful distance from the open hatch, and twisting interestingly, in an attempt to see inside.

"The Clutch use the Electron Substitution Drive," Theo reminded her.

"As we learned at school," Kara agreed. "I don't recall much more detail than that—certainly nothing about engines, or coils, or fuel."

Theo frowned.

"Clutch travel through dense space, by choice," she said, trying to remember the textbook on drives and motivation protocols. Surprisingly, though this was exactly the sort of thing that interested *Bechimo*, bond-space was empty of his presence; empty of any sudden manifestation of an article or schematic ...

"I recall that," Kara said. "And also the assertion that the drive produces an effect where the ship simultaneously exists at the beginning of its route, and the end."

"There was something about entanglement, too," Theo said, and shook her head. "I'd have to look it up."

"And I. But even granted the lack of coils or Struven units, it must propel itself in some manner!"

She began a slow walk around the boulder, and Theo let her go, straining in her turn to see inside the ship, and getting an impression of smooth rock walls, and lighting that was both dim, and subtly *off*. The shelf she glimpsed opposite the hatch might have been a board.

Or, she allowed, it might have just been a shelf carved out of the rock.

"*Bechimo*," she said, in bond-space.

"Yes, Captain?"

Theo sighed quietly. Apparently she was in disgrace. Well, she'd sort it out later.

"Would you please do a complete scan of this ship? It's going to bother Kara for the rest of her life if she can't figure out how it flies."

"Certainly, Captain," *Bechimo* said, and withdrew.

Definitely in disgrace. She wondered what she'd done, then put it out of her mind as the sound of the gate working brought her about.

A car swept up the drive, and pulled over. The back doors opened, and two pilots exited.

Two *young* pilots exited.

Theo bit her lip, remembering that Kara and Hevelin were witnesses. These two pilots therefore were not her father and Val Con's mother, but young cousins, come to Surebleak, to throw their luck in with the rest of Clan Korval.

Kor Vid yos'Phelium and Daaneka tey'Doshi, Theo told herself, her stomach tight. Kor Vid yos'Phelium and—

Behind her, Hevelin screamed.

* * *

Daav had the door open before the car had fairly stopped. Aelliana was out nearly as quickly, pausing until he reached her side.

He could scarcely blame her for hesitating, for it was a strange scene, indeed, that confronted them.

In the foreground was Theo, looking as ill-tempered as he had ever seen her. Directly behind her was what was surely a Clutch ship with its hatch up. Its resemblance to the ship in which Edger had transported them to their meeting with the Clutch Elders was meager: While Edger's ship could have easily been mistaken for a small moon on holiday, this present object appeared to be the merest asteroid, unaccountably come to rest in the center of Korval's drive.

There were no Clutch persons immediately evident, which was, Daav admitted to himself, something of a relief. Theo had obviously been left to guide them, and perhaps to impart something approaching information.

There was a flicker of movement as another pilot came 'round the far side of the rocky vessel and moved toward Theo.

Daav, Aelliana said inside his head. *That norbear. Is—*

The driveway morphed into a narrow alley, dark air glittering with icy flakes, the footing treacherous, snow-covered, and before them an angry mob, voices rough with fear and rage. There—Aelliana pelting directly into the thick of it, skidding as she gained the side of the pilot crouching low, his voice broken and pleading—pushing him back and swinging 'round to confront the throng.

A stone arced out of the crowd, and Daav heard his own voice, in the mode of Command, ordering—

"Enough! Hevelin, you're going to deafen the whole house!"

The images blew away like so many snowflakes. Daav shook his head, found that he had hold of Aelliana's hand—or she, of his—and that the order had come from Theo, who held the norbear in her arms, while the other pilot had a hand to her head.

"Enough!" Theo repeated. "You hurt Kara, is that what you wanted to do?"

There came a sense of contrition, much muted, and a scent perhaps of mint, to soothe abused heads.

So much, I fear, for secrecy, Aelliana said, stepping forward.

We may yet come about, Daav answered, keeping pace with her.

"Well met, Cousin Theo," he called. "May one inquire? Does the pilot require aid?"

"Kara?" Theo put the norbear down and turned to the other, her posture eloquent of distress. "Do you want a 'doc?"

Kara drew a shaky breath, and lifted her head.

"What *was* that?" she asked, somewhat faintly.

Theo put an arm around her waist.

"Hevelin," she started . . .

"It would seem that the norbear believes he knows us," Aelliana said, glaring down at the norbear in question, who was now at her feet, standing tall on his back legs and stretching toward her, clearly wishing to be picked up.

"He thinks he knows a lot of people," Kara said, sounding somewhat less breathless, though she did not seem disposed to shake off Theo's support. "I have never heard him—scream. And the—" she shook her head and focused on Aelliana.

"Forgive me, pilot, but he *must* know you. That memory . . ."

"Yes, well." Aelliana sighed and tucked her hands into her belt, shaking her head at her furry supplicant.

"No, rogue; I will *not* take you up. We are called by the delm; and that business has precedence."

"Yes!" Kara said, with shaky enthusiasm. "Do you see, Hevelin? Your necessities are not the most important, always."

Daav hunkered down on his heels, the better to look into dark norbear eyes.

Hevelin turned from Aelliana, and put a hand on Daav's wrist. A sequence formed behind his eyes—not the mob this time, thank the gods, but the bridge of *Ride the Luck*, a considerably less-grey Hevelin climbing out of the case to confront Aelliana, her face a mixture of laughing disbelief and anger that her ship had been placed in danger.

"Yes, I quite see," he said, softly, but loud enough for Theo and Kara, too, to hear him. "Assuredly, we must dream together. But dreaming must wait upon our delm's desires. That is reality, my friend. If reality moves in such a way that we meet again after the delm has done with us, then will we three dream."

"In the meanwhile," Aelliana added, sternly; "you would do well to refrain from deafening your comrades, and perhaps show them a little care."

Hevelin sighed, and dropped to all four feet. Another wave of contrition spread out from him, and another cooling breath of mint.

Daav came to his feet. Kara had stepped out of Theo's embrace, her brows pulled together, as she looked from Hevelin to Aelliana—to him.

"The delm sent?" Daav prompted Theo.

"She did, yes."

Theo motioned toward the rock-ship.

"Emissary Twelve arrived, in haste. She says she's from the Clutch Elders."

She paused.

"It seems like she's under strain. Not only the Jumps, but—I got the idea that maybe the Elders aren't easy to work for. She has questions and she needs answers."

"And it is assumed that I have answers," he said lightly, looking to Aelliana. "What a treat for us, Pilot."

"Indeed."

He turned back to Theo.

"The delm and Emissary Twelve are where, just now?"

"In the garden. Emissary Twelve thought maybe she'd take the Tree to the Elders. I think Miri—the delm—is letting her see for herself how much of a problem that could be."

"Very wise," Aelliana said gravely, and gave him a nod. "We to the Tree Court and the delm, Pilot."

"So it would seem. Thank you, Cousin. Pilot Kara, forgive us, please, for our part in your distress."

Kara shook her head.

"There is nothing to forgive," she said, and dropped her gaze to Hevelin, who was sitting calmly on the drive, listening avidly, so Daav greatly feared.

"It so strange," Kara continued, looking to Theo. "It's not like him to make such an error."

"He does make errors of *kind*, sometimes," Theo said carefully. "He showed the Pathfinders my father, after they'd given him a—what was it? An M-soldier?"

Kara sighed, brows still tight, clearly unconvinced.

Aelliana bowed.

"Pilot Kara, I am Daaneka tey'Doshi, and this my co-pilot is Kor Vid yos'Phelium. We are at your service."

Kara bowed.

"Kara ven'Arith, Pilots. I am pleased to meet you."

A breeze flowed, quick and green, over them, where a moment before the day had been windless.

"We *are* wanted," Daav said to Aelliana.

"So I see. No, Cousin Theo, we know the way. Please, care for your comrades."

She strode off, Daav at her side; the green breeze harrying them along.

When they were passed through the garden gate, out of sight and presumably out of earshot, Kara turned back to Theo, her brows drawn in a deep frown.

"Hevelin does *not* make those kinds of mistakes," she said, flatly.

Theo looked at the norbear, who was sitting on the driveway, apparently deep in thought. Nothing came to her from him—no commentary, no sense of participation—nothing. He might've been just some random furry creature that had wandered out of the garden and onto the drive.

"Theo?" Kara said.

Theo sighed, and turned to meet Kara's eyes.

"No," she said. "Hevelin *doesn't* make those kind of mistakes. He did meet those pilots before—and I can't tell you anything else, because it's . . . family business, and not mine to tell."

She expected temper—Kara *had* a temper, though she was 'way better than Theo was about keeping it under control. Still—she'd been assaulted by a norbear; lied to by pilots; and gotten worse than no explanation for any of it from her friend and her captain. It was enough to make anybody angry, in Theo's opinion.

Kara, though . . .

Kara actually seemed . . . relieved. Her face relaxed, and she sighed.

"If it is in the clan, then of course you must keep it so," she said.

That seemed to be a match-up with Kara's opinion that Val Con and Miri were Theo's delm—which they weren't—and Theo was about to take that on again when it occurred to her that she *didn't* have an explanation other than "clan secret," or "Delm's Word" that wasn't an outright lie.

Half-truth, then, she thought; compromise, if we can't have consensus.

"Now, then, sir!"

Kara strolled over to where Hevelin sat, still and shuttered. She knelt on the drive facing him and, after a moment, Theo joined her.

"Hevelin," Kara said softly; "the pilots had pressing business; their delm had called them to duty."

There was a stir; perhaps even a sigh.

In the space right behind her eyes, Theo saw, illuminated as if by a sun, the two pilots—very nearly the first "dream" Hevelin shared with everyone he met.

Two pilots, male and female, dark and light, sardonic and sweet-faced; each standing well within the other's personal space, clearly partners, comfortable with themselves and their arrangement.

An old memory, since the dark pilot was Father before he had come to Delgado to take the Gallowglass Chair. An old memory, and Father a young man—yet still older than the pilot who, with his partner, had just passed down the drive on their way to the Tree Court and their delm.

She felt a sort of a light pinch near her ear, drawing her attention back to the dream of the two pilots.

"Yes," she said, carefully. "That is Daav yos'Phelium, who was also Jen Sar Kiladi. He's my father, and he's Val Con's father. The other pilot is Aelliana Caylon, Val Con's mother."

Beside her, she heard Kara draw a sharp breath.

The brilliant memory faded, leaving behind an impression like chilly fog. Out of it, another dream formed—of the two pilots who had just left them: male and female, dark and light, sardonic and sweet; each standing well within the other's personal space, clearly partners, comfortable with themselves and their arrangement.

"Yes," Theo said, even more carefully. "The best I can tell you is what they told you themselves. Those are Kor Vid yos'Phelium and Daaneka tey'Doshi." She took a breath.

"You heard me tell Kara that anything else is Clan Korval business."

There was a burst of protest at that. Hevelin was not a wet-eared kit; *he* could keep a secret! He had *many* secrets.

"We all have secrets," Theo said. "But, see, this secret isn't mine, and it isn't yours. It's *their* secret, and they're the only ones who can decide to share it—and with who."

There was a long pause, then a very specific sending of the corner of Theo's apartment, where Mr. pel'Kana had set up the comfortable little nest.

"It's been a long shift," Theo agreed.

She rolled to her feet, and held a hand down to Kara.

"Something tells me I'd better check in with the crew."

Kara accepted the hand and the boost to her feet.

"Possibly Clarence will have some small interest in events," she said dryly.

Theo laughed, and bent down to hoist Hevelin to her shoulder.

"Yeah," she said. "Maybe he will."

They crossed the drive in companionable silence; the door opening as they approached.

"Thank you, Jeeves," Theo said, turning toward the stairway.

"You are welcome. There is an urgent message from Joyita waiting."

Theo stopped, and blinked.

"Urgent?" she repeated, suddenly recalling *Bechimo's* uncharacteristic silence on a subject he found fascinating. But, he'd have said something, if there'd been a problem. Wouldn't he?

"If this message is urgent—" she began, as Kara lifted Hevelin to her own shoulder.

"It has only just arrived," Jeeves told her. "Will you hear it?"

"Yes."

"Captain," Joyita's voice carried an unaccustomed edge of irritation. "Surebleak Portmaster requests your presence in her office immediately, regarding the drones we set in Surebleak orbit." There was a short pause. "She did not sound happy."

Theo looked at Kara.

Kara looked at Theo.

Theo sighed.

"Jeeves, please ask Tommy if he's available to drive me to the port. Also, may I speak to Joyita?"

"Certainly," Jeeves said. "Joyita, Captain Waitley wishes to speak with you."

"Captain?"

Theo sighed again, and closed her eyes.

"Please tell Surebleak Portmaster that I have received her message and will be with her as quickly as possible."

"Yes, Captain," said Joyita, followed by a subtle click, as if he had closed a connection.

Kara shifted.

"Shall I come with you, as crew representative?" Kara asked. "The entire ship had agreed on—"

Theo shook her head.

"The portmaster will take it as given that the captain speaks for the ship." she said. "You and Hevelin bring the crew up to date. I should be back soon."

She produced a slight grin.

"How long can it take to pay a fine, after all?"

Chapter Four

Surebleak

Jelaza Kazone

Emissary Twelve, Val Con thought, as he and Miri escorted that middling large person through the garden gate and down the path that would lead them, roundabout, to the Tree Court.

Emissary Twelve was something of a curiosity. Val Con had spent some time as a hopeful Scout, living with Edger and the Knife Clan of Middle River. He had learned that Edger represented one end of the Clutch spectrum—open to new experience, and able to entertain a certain tolerance—not to say fondness—for humankind. On the other end of that spectrum stood the brood mother, who was inclined to view anything different as dangerous, and to meet all perceived danger with deadly force.

Others of Edger's clan had fallen somewhere between the two extremes of *T'carais* and brood mother, with Edger's heir, the young *T'caraisiana'ab* standing closest to his progenitor, and Selector standing nearest the brood mother, though they had scarcely been shoulder-to-shoulder, and room for two or three well-shelled Clutch between them.

He had not, during his time with the Middle River Clan, been summoned, or shown to, the Elders, though Edger had twice been called to attend that august body. It had been Handler who had instructed the brother of the *T'carais* in the history, function, and physiology of the Old Ones.

However, as befit one of the clan who also stood high in the esteem of the *T'carais*, he had several times walked the caverns in company with Edger, Handler, and, on one notable occasion, with Selector.

What had made that particular tour so notable had been a minor rockslide, not so much blocking their way as narrowing their access. Val Con could have skipped over the fall with ease, and despite his shell, Selector might have passed with only a very little more trouble.

Still, after a long study and a series of notes sung very nearly below Val Con's ability to hear, Selector had turned, gathering his brother's brother to him with a curt wave of a three-fingered hand.

"We will go by another path," he said. "Stay close and do not wander."

The admonition not to wander had been fair enough, and indeed he *had* stayed close. Which is how he happened to enter the cavern on Selector's heels before that person checked his stride, muttering something under his breath.

Thus prompted, Val Con had looked about him with some interest, and seen, not tender crystals, nor yet full-grown blades, ready for inspection and selection.

No.

The cavern, chilly by even Clutch standards, had contained . . .

Eggs.

Dozens, hundreds of large, dark eggs, their surfaces faintly iridescent, even in the dimness, as if they had been dipped in oil.

Or as if they were coated in ice.

Selector let his breath out in a long, slow sigh.

"You will follow exactly in my footsteps. You will touch nothing. You will say nothing. You will *think* nothing. Do you understand me?"

"Yes," Val Con breathed, and did as he was told.

After they had finally gained the room of newly grown knives from which Selector was to choose only those most perfect, Val Con had watched carefully, and had taken care not to ask any questions—not for a lack of curiosity, but because he did not wish to agitate his brother's brother any further.

Later, he sat alone by the hearth, telling over his trove of questions, seeking to frame at least one which would not be found offensive, yet still elicit an informative answer.

And, while he sat mulling, Edger came to him.

"You have questions, Brother. Ask."

"Who are they . . . meant to be?" Val Con said after a moment; not his best question, but the thing he was most curious to learn. "Those waiting in the cold?"

"Gently asked," Edger said. "They are *meant*, my brother, to be what you may call *soldiers*. They are our defense, our offense, and our shame. We cause them to be born . . . rarely, and only against an enemy which has chosen to contest us.

"We call them Short Lives. We call them Destroyers. We call them the Quick and the Dead. As they are now, we call them the Unrequired, and we hope that name grows no longer."

"The Yxtrang," Val Con said then, recalling his history; "they run from Clutch ships."

"They do, now. When first we encountered them, they were of a mind to conquer us. We have several times been required to answer the Yxtrang with the Short Lives. They forget, after a certain passage of time, and the Unrequired must be waked again."

"Short Lives?" Val Con asked then, and was answered with another sigh.

"Once the eggs are quickened, they are born within hours. Within a day, they have their full strength and all of their skills.

"Within three revolutions, those who have survived the task for which they were born . . . die, shell-less, nameless, and unmourned by any clan."

Shell-less, Val Con thought now, and a terrifying warrior within a day of hatching. Such a one, perhaps, would look very like Emissary Twelve.

In the office at the port, Val Con took a hard breath against rising dismay.

The Elders were not physically quick, but he was not at all surprised to learn that they had the ability to monitor insults to the fabric of the universe itself. The Elders would not—could not—come themselves, but they could send a newly born and fully capable Emissary, very quickly, indeed.

Miri paused, then, bringing his attention back to the garden. They had reached one of the last wide spots in the path, and she had paused to speak to Jeeves.

"Best wait for us here," she said. "No sense you having to bushwhack your way down the path."

"Yes, Korval," Jeeves said, which was, Val Con thought, very nice in him.

Emissary Twelve scarcely seemed to mark the fact that they had left their escort behind.

Miri led the way down the path, Val Con walking with her. They breathed in the scent of leaf and loam, of flowers and—

Miri, the garden, Emissary Twelve—vanished in a blare of static; his ears roared, and cleared to hear with remarkable clarity, a large, calm, and very familiar voice.

"Road Boss yos'Phelium, Team Leader Soreya Kasveini of TerraTrade Survey is here to conduct an interview. Are you available to her?"

Gods, TerraTrade. He blanked the screen on his desk, closed his eyes, and visualized the Scout's Rainbow, feeling his heartbeat slow, and his breathing steady. His temper . . . well. Uncle Er Thom has used to say that manners were both one's first defense, and first offense, had he not?

"I am pleased to speak with Team Leader Kasveini," he said, untruthfully. "Please, bring her in to me."

* * *

Val Con was on to something, Miri thought, feeling his concentration deepen. Maybe he'd actually met somebody like Emissary Twelve, back when he'd been living with Edger's clan.

She hoped he had remembered something useful, because Emissary Twelve was starting to make her nervous. There was something more than just a little not-quite-right about—

He was gone; vanished between one step and the next one, leaving her alone inside her head.

She reached out, in a way she couldn't have described, if asked, but which was as natural as extending her hand. At the end of her mental fingers, she found him; his pattern edgy and ill-tempered, with a metallic patina of what might be formal manners overlying it all.

If she had to guess—and it looked like she was going to have to—she'd figure that the TerraTrade survey team had made it to the Road Boss's office. She took a deep breath, disengaged, and damn' near ran into Emissary Twelve, who had frozen so completely she didn't seem to breathe. She was staring into the shrubberies that overgrew the pathway.

"Is there a problem?" Miri asked.

The saucer eyes never moved, but the chest did, rising and falling in one careful breath.

"There are predators hiding inside those leaves."

"Predators? I—"

She closed her mouth, and looked harder at the bush that seemed to be the greatest source of concern. There, among the leaves, were two pair of glowing green eyes.

"Cats," she said; "just cats."

"Predators," Emissary Twelve insisted.

"Well . . . yes. They hunt *small* things," Miri said; "pests. Mostly rodents."

"They will not attack?"

"They have no reason to attack," Miri said. "They might follow along, though. They're curious."

"Sentient?" demanded Emissary Twelve.

Miri blinked, then shrugged.

"Let's go with yes," she said; "but they're really self-absorbed."

Emissary Twelve shifted her gaze to Miri's face.

"If they attack, I will defend myself," she said flatly.

Oh, no; Miri'd seen Clutch move when they were defending themselves. Cats were fast, but they weren't *that* fast. Besides which . . .

"If you *think* they're attacking, you'll defer to me," she said, reaching into High Liaden for just the right icy inflection. "The cats are part of this household, and they are under the protection of the delm. Understood?"

There was a long-ish pause, eyes open and staring, then a blink.

"Understood."

"Good." Miri turned and started walking again. It had seemed a good idea to leave Jeeves—to leave Jeeves's chassis—back where the path was more open. Now, though, she regretted the loss of a visible display of authority. Her previous experience of Clutch hadn't encompassed anything like this nervy, cautious person. Of course, Edger was too tall, and too well-shelled, to be concerned about the possibility of an attack by house-cats. And she'd never seen Edger, or Sheather, or any of the marketing research team anywhere near the end of their resources.

Even Watcher—well, Watcher hadn't *liked* them, but she hadn't gotten the sense that he'd been a *danger* to them.

The path curved around the big bush that she thought of the gateway to the Tree Court.

"Here we are," she said, over her shoulder. "Mind the footing."

The Tree was in a rare good mood, she thought, as she picked her way over the surface roots toward the massive trunk. The breeze was warm, with a faint edge of brisk; and there was ozone in the mix, which wasn't usual. On the other hand, maybe the Tree was adjusting the air to their guest's preferred sort, as a courtesy.

She paused halfway between the end of the path and the Tree itself, waiting for Emissary Twelve, who came to her side, and stopped, looking up.

"I cannot escort that to the Elders," she said, sounding tired and irritable and more than ready to call it a day.

"That's right," Miri said easily. "It took the largest vessel the Clutch own to move it—and the house—from Liad to this location. I'm pretty sure the Tree'll be pleased to give you all the information it has about the mending of the flaw in the universe. Edger had perfect recall, as far as I could ever tell, and Sheather, too. Is your memory that good?"

"*My* memory is not impaired," Emissary Twelve snapped, which Miri chose to read it as just fact, rather than a comment on Ren Zel's shortcomings.

"That's good, then. All you have to do is listen—and remember."

"Listen," Emissary Twelve repeated, flatly.

"Right. How we do it, is we put our hands flat against the trunk—here, I'll show you."

She stepped up to the trunk, receiving an impression of amused welcome as the brisk little breeze ruffled her hair.

"Good-morning to you, too," she said. "This is Emissary Twelve. She'd like you to tell her about the flaw in the universe, and what you and Ren Zel did to close it. Are you willing?"

There was a stirring of pride in the air, which Miri took for *yes*.

She turned to Emissary Twelve, who was standing a few steps too far from the trunk.

"Gotta come closer," she said, and the Clutch obeyed, reluctantly, Miri thought.

"Right," she said, and turned back to the Tree. Closing her eyes, she placed both hands against the trunk.

The bark warmed under her palms, and she felt a rush of affectionate greenness. Sighing, she leaned into the feeling.

"Your turn," she said, without opening her eyes.

She felt the Tree greet the guest—warm and open, but without overt affection. Behind her eyes, she saw a glittering golden expanse opening on all sides, and flowing away—to a dark and inimical shadow at the edge of the field of gold. And where the shadow touched, gold blackened and shriveled.

Wind blew in a frigid gale from the shadow, a wind that carried the stench of rotting vegetation, and old blood.

More gold blackened, until there came a flash of pure energy, a counter-wind lashed into being, and—

Somewhere, somebody screamed—a terrible gargling shriek. Shadow and gold alike snapped out of Miri's awareness, and the bark went cold and inert under her hands.

She spun, one hand snatching at her hideaway—and falling away as she dropped to her knees beside the inert form of Emissary Twelve.

* * *

The breeze had become insistent, pushing them into what might have been an ill-advised trot, had the overgrowth not obligingly moved aside, rather than entangling their feet, or whipping back to strike an unprotected cheek.

His legs being longer, Daav came into the Tree Court one step ahead of Aelliana—and slammed to a halt, throwing an arm out to stop her, as well. The breeze that had harried them died in the same instant, as they surveyed the scene before them.

One Clutch Turtle measuring its relatively meager length on the ground at the foot of the Tree.

One Korval delm on her knees beside said Clutch, a slender hand on the shell-less breast, above the woven leather harness.

On either side of the delm of Korval, her honor guard; two cats—one white and fluffy, the other sleek and striped—poised over ready toes, considering the downed visitor with what could only be disdain.

"What," Aelliana said quietly, "has occurred here?"

The kneeling delm lifted her head, but any explanation she might have expected to embark upon was lost to the Tree's sudden and succinct sequence of images.

"Pretty much that's it," Miri said, when the Tree's narrative came to an end. "Mind you, I was in the loop, standing right next to her. It was . . . intense, but not overwhelming."

She gave a wry smile.

"To me, anyway."

She sat back on her heels, moving her hand from the Clutch to the back of the cat at her right.

"This is Emissary Twelve, by the way," she added, and shook her head, her gaze wandering back to the fallen. "Something not quite right with Emissary Twelve, if you ask me. She's edgy and outta temper; threatened to murder the cats if they tried to pull anything."

She looked back up.

"Edger got along just fine with cats."

"Possibly Edger had prior experience of cats," Aelliana suggested.

"Maybe. Val Con—I felt him get hold of something, right before he—I'm guessing the survey team came 'round for their interview . . . And now here I am thinking maybe it's best Emissary Twelve here is taking a nice nap."

Another wry smile.

"Time limit on that, though."

Aelliana strolled into the center of the court, and sat down on the grass, facing Miri across the supine form of the Clutch. After a moment, Daav joined her.

"If it can be told," he said, using his chin to point at the sleeper; "what does Emissary Twelve want with Kor Vid yos'Phelium?"

Miri sighed.

"You gotta understand that Kor Vid's the Emissary's third choice.

"First, she wanted—*immediately*, she said, in a way that sounded even faster than standard human-issue immediately—Ren Zel, destroyer of the universe. 'course, that hit a stone wall, with him and Anthora at the Healers. She got real put off when I told her that he was already forgetting what he'd done, and might not be able to tell the Elders—Emissary Twelve is sent straight from Elders—anything more than they already know."

"What do the Elders know, I wonder," Aelliana said.

Miri looked at her owlishly.

"That there was a flaw in the fabric of the universe which they'd been observing for some while. She didn't phrase it this way, but the impression I have from Emissary Twelve is that their noses are outta joint because Ren Zel fixed it."

"They have him as *destroyer* of the universe? It would seem to me that his name ought to be adjusted to include *redeemer* of the universe," Daav said.

"Yeah, the Elders apparently see that Ren Zel saved one of two possible universes, and the other one died because of it. The way I do the math, that makes him savior and destroyer in the same sentence, but apparently the Elders are peeved."

"Ah," said Daav.

The fluffy white cat stretched high on pink toes and walked across Emissary Twelve to claim Aelliana's lap.

"One wonders what the Elders were intending to do about the situation," Aelliana said, stroking her sudden tenant. "Before Ren Zel won the game, that is."

"Emissary Twelve didn't say. What she did say, since she hadn't been given any orders about people inconveniently losing their memories, was that she'd take Daav yos'Phelium, instead. Seems he promised, if the Elders had more questions, that he'd return to answer them."

Aelliana turned to look at him.

"Really, *van'chela*. However did you come to be so inept?"

He moved his shoulders.

"It seemed unlikely that the Elders would be able to produce further questions in my remaining lifetime. Also, they were pushing strongly for guarantees, and a willingness to answer further questions mollified them, so that I was able to extract myself."

He frowned.

"I note that Emissary Twelve has shaved her dice," he said slowly. "Daav yos'Phelium guaranteed that he would return to answer questions about Korval's relocation, the condition of the Tree, and the state of the ship which had been placed at Korval's service. He promised nothing regarding the salvation or destruction of universes."

"It would seem that the delm is not eager to accommodate the Elders," Aelliana said. "At least so far as sending clan members to them."

Miri looked down, seeming surprised to find the brown-striped cat had climbed onto her knee and was lounging at his ease, purring.

"Well, assuming that the Elders are annoyed with us, the delm's official position is that we're naturally grieved to have offended an ally, but we're not sending any of ours for them to vent their spleen on."

Aelliana inclined her head.

"Do we know for certain," Daav said, "that a universe was destroyed?"

Miri sighed.

"For the purposes of this conversation, let's assume that two universes went in, one came out—just like the Elders are saying. Frankly, I'm not feeling up to considering the melding of two universes, or multiple cascading time warps, or anything else that needs more math to think about than a merc captain's likely to have on her at this hour of the day."

"Simplicity serves us best," Daav agreed. "So, then; Ren Zel preserved our universe, which action caused the demise of a second. A wise choice; I could have made no better."

"Given that the delm does not care to send any of the clan to the Clutch, how was the problem of Emissary Twelve to be solved?" Aelliana asked.

Miri waved a hand over her head, possibly indicating the Tree.

"My idea was that maybe we could do a substitution that would satisfy everybody. Emissary Twelve owned to having a non-defective memory, so I figured if the Tree told her what happened, then she could tell the Elders, and nobody had to be disrupted."

"Except that Emissary Twelve could not accept the Tree's sending." Aelliana shook her head. "There must be a way 'round that."

From above them, high and away in the Tree's branches, came a sharp snap and the sound of something falling, swiftly, through leaf and branch.

Miri extended her hand, fingers closing around the pod when it struck her palm.

Daav sat up straight, ice running his spine.

"Tell me that is *not*—"

Miri shook her head.

"It's for Emissary Twelve, all right. And I'm glad to know that I'm not the only one who thinks it's a bad idea."

Chapter Five

Sureblak Port

Captain Waitley wasn't quite what Portmaster Liu had been expecting.

No, scratch that, in a lot of ways, Captain Waitley was *exactly* what Portmaster Liu had been expecting: short for a Terran, tall for a Liaden, lean for the height she did have; shoulders showing attitude under a Jump jacket older and bigger than she was. Whatever else she was—and recklessly negligent wasn't off the table, in Portmaster Liu's not-exactly-objective opinion—Theo Waitley was definitely a member of Boss Conrad's extended family, Clan Korval. Portmaster Liu had been spending a lot of time lately with the Boss and the Boss's little brother, the Road Boss; she knew the family look when she saw it.

What did surprise her was the wild scramble of wispy fair hair, the pale skin, and the obvious frown. Captain Waitley was ticked off, which was fair enough. What was interesting, though, was how plain she let that bad temper show.

On several occasions over the course of their profitable, if not exactly placid, relationship, Boss Conrad had reason to be annoyed with Portmaster Liu, which she'd never known from his face. Crisp over-politeness was the first clue, followed by frozen good manners, and a toxic increase in irony levels, if whatever was making him peevish didn't subside straight off.

Well, and maybe Captain Waitley had found that a frank and open display of temper got her the results she wanted. It probably took a fair amount of practice to perfect Boss Conrad's style.

"Portmaster Liu, I'm sorry to have kept you waiting," the captain said—well, snapped. "You wanted to talk with me about the drones we dropped off?"

She blinked.

Got right down to the business at hand, did Captain Waitley, without even so much as an inquiry into the Portmaster's general health and the state of the port. Nothing rude about it—a classic Terran approach, really. Some of the kids attached to Conrad's family were taking up the Terran mode, from what she'd seen and heard, so—fair enough, again.

"I appreciate you coming so quick," she answered. "Good timing, as it happens. I got a survey team on my hands. They'll be wanting to have my attention in about twenty minutes. So we'll need to settle our business fairly smart."

Captain Waitley nodded briskly.

"I won't waste your time. I've come to pay my fine."

Well, now—the fine. On the one hand, it was good that she knew she'd be having to pay a fine and wasn't making the smallest suggestion that it could be lost, friendly-like, in the paperwork.

You'd think, though, given a captain with a reputation of a certain kind, attached to a family that valued its ships more than the lives of their children—you'd think that captain'd consider the fine—hefty as it was—the least of her problems.

Which maybe meant that Captain Waitley hadn't quite reasoned her way into a full set of understandings.

Well, Portmaster Liu thought, consciously bringing herself taller in the chair; this'll be fun.

"Have a seat, Captain," she said, nodding at the smaller chair by the side of her desk.

Captain Waitley's frown got frownier, but she sat down, civilized enough, and, as a seeming afterthought, folded her hands on her knee.

"The fine now," the portmaster said, forcing herself to talk easy in the face of that visible increase in bad temper. "You'll take care of that with the bursar. I'll point you in his direction after we get done talking about the citation."

Space black eyes blinked.

"Citation?" she repeated, real quiet.

Right, thought the portmaster. *This* was the street Captain Waitley was willing to die on. Money was only money—well, Portmaster Liu could agree on that point, most times. But a citation, now—that was an assault against *honor*—and, the little gods of nuts 'n bolts save her, she *might've* just let it go with a stern talking-to, rather than fight that fight with one of Conrad's own, but—

"Citation?" Captain Waitley said again, even quieter.

"That's right," Portmaster Liu said, giving the thing weight with a brisk nod. "We're laying a *grava citajo*—a major citation—for violation of spaceway protocol for one Standard Year against your personal license, and a six-monther against your ship."

"That's . . . steep," Captain Waitley observed, which as a response was a lot milder than the portmaster had braced herself for, considering that it was going to be *damned* spensive in terms of hazard fees and dangerous-docking levies. Small trader was gonna *feel* that.

"It is," she agreed. "And I'm sorry to say that I can't let either one slide off the table."

Another blink; the frown fading into thoughtfulness.

"Aren't you the portmaster?"

Quick on the pick-up—well, that was the family, too, grandpa to babe-in-arms.

"That's right," she said equitably. "I'm the portmaster."

"Well, then, why *can't*?" the captain asked, which was a reasonable enough question. "I admit that we—theoretically—imperiled traffic. I have no quarrel with being fined. The drone didn't cause an accident; it's gone by now, and even if it had collided with a ship, the most they would have thought was they'd caught a patch of dust. Still—you're the portmaster, and I was out of line. We agree."

She took a deep breath, visibly settling into being calm, and Portmaster Liu took a similar breath, in solidarity.

"Typical offenses that merit a *grava citajo* are: law-breaking, port-breaking, child-stealing, illegal dealings, piloting to endanger—"

Girl knew her regs, plain enough. Portmaster Liu held up a hand, palm out.

"You're right. I'm calling down a blizzard where a squall would do, like they say out in the city. Between us, if you'd dropped your little party favor in my shipping lanes on any other day, I'd've fined you, dressed you down like you'd never worn clothes before, and we'd've parted on good terms.

"But you happened to pull this stupid stunt at the exact same time we got a TerraTrade survey on-port, trying their best to figure out how to hold back that upgrade you might've heard Boss Conrad is so set on us getting."

Another frown, and a speculative look.

"You're saying that you not only have to go by the book, you've got to go by the strictest reading possible, or the survey team will find cause to withhold," Captain Waitley said with a slight nod. "I see that; I don't have a problem with the fine. I won't like it, but knowing the reasons, I'll even swallow the six monther against the ship, but—"

Portmaster Liu held up her hand again, and glanced at the clock on the wall.

"There's another factor that you're not taking into account, Captain. This is gonna sound brusque, but I'm getting short on time. The reason the survey team is looking *so hard* for reasons to deny this port its upgrade is because of what happened at Solcintra. At least one member of the team has it as his stated opinion that Clan Korval is outright pirates and all Surebleak Port deserves is a Do Not Stop until such time as you and yours leaves the planet."

She paused, and tipped her head slightly.

"Pardon?" she asked politely.

Captain Waitley shook her head.

"Nothing; sorry. Why are they even bothering to survey, if that's their opinion?"

"It's only *one* opinion out of a possible three. The other members of the team state that they've brought no preconceptions to the survey. Which might be so, but even if it *is* so doesn't necessarily mean that TerraTrade thinks the same. In which case, they've got the team doing the survey so's to have the record full and proper, and no questions, this time. Nor any appeals."

Captain Waitley's frown was back; she fluttered her fingers, pilot-sign for *go on.*

"Right. So, what I have to make plain as the snow in front of your nose is that the portmaster's office doesn't put up with any kind or size of shenanigans, and that we're particularly keeping a *very* close eye on the members of Clan Korval. Any of 'em step outta line, and they get slapped, fast and hard."

She took a hard breath, aware that she'd been getting a little emphatic, and finished it off quiet.

"On account of this is *Surebleak Port*, not Port Korval—nowhere even close."

There was a little bit of silence, which she didn't interrupt, despite the time.

"I'm not a member of Clan Korval," Captain Waitley said eventually. "I'm a citizen of Delgado."

Right or wrong, Portmaster Liu couldn't help but feel some sympathy. The captain was doing a good enough job of holding on to her temper, and working through the possibles, as clean and crisp as if the whole of it was a problem out of ethics class. Unfortunately . . .

"That might work as a dodge on another day, Captain," she said kindly; "but I'm betting the survey team's not ignorant of the fact that you're the Road Boss's sister. You being a Terran and a citizen of Delgado—all that's aside. You're family, even if you aren't clan."

There was a longish silence.

"I pulled an extra-heavy fine and two *grava citajos because* I'm Val Con's sister," Captain Waitley repeated, seeming like she just wanted to be sure she had the info right.

"That's right, Captain. I'm real sorry about it, but we got a lot riding on getting this upgraded certification. Ain't just your family wants it. All Surebleak *needs* it."

Deep breath, then; muscles visibly loosened. Captain Waitley inclined her head *just* like Boss Conrad would have it, and said, in an over-dry voice.

"Thank you again for seeing me, Port Master. I'll leave you now to your business. If you'll just point me toward the bursar's office?"

"Sure thing; it's right on the way out, at the bottom of the stairs." She hesitated, eyeing the captain as she got to her feet.

"You take care now, hear?"

* * *

"Because the idea of an open supply system from the port throughout the city and to the settlements beyond the city is a relatively new one, the Road Boss does, as you see, hold open office hours. Our object is not only to answer questions regarding the rules of the road, and to share information, but also to learn from the native population. We have had valuable input regarding the history of the main supply routes—of which the Port Road is merely the longest—how the costs of maintenance and patrol were apportioned before the colony was abandoned by the Gilmour Agency, and the local culture devolved.

"The Road Boss and others of the Council of Bosses are working in committee to identify the secondary routes, assess their value, and to produce a timeline for the establishment—I should say, re-establishment—of those routes, in cases where it is warranted."

"Then the Road Boss's office primarily benefits the city?" asked Soreya Kasveini.

"Supply flows in both directions," Val Con said patiently. "Goods move from the port to the city. Likewise, goods and workers move from the city to the port. It is a symbiosis; the success of each depends upon the vitality of both."

"The file on this office which was provided by the portmaster indicates that there are protocols in place for ensuring that the Port Road remains open. One of those protocols involves armed enforcement. Does your office employ soldiers? Mercenaries, perhaps?"

Val Con took a careful breath, and produced a Terran smile for the benefit of the interviewer.

"Surebleak has been enjoying a period of population growth. Among those who have chosen to establish a base here are a number of active mercenary units. In addition, Surebleak has in its native population a significant number of retired military. This is to say that, should it become necessary to keep the Port Road open by force of arms, then the means to implement that protocol is close to hand."

He moved his shoulders, and looked wry.

"Speaking as Road Boss, I do not think we will find any necessity to use such means to secure the road. We are fortunate, that those who live in the city largely see the Port Road as a benefit. There is some complaint with regard to the usage fees, but it is traditional, after all, to be aggrieved by the fees."

Team Leader Kasveini actually produced a smile of her own.

"It is, isn't it?" she said, and sighed, looking up to meet his eyes.

"What is your estimation," she said, "of the possibility of an attempt to close the road from the port side?"

He lifted an eyebrow.

"An invasion, you mean?"

"Something along those lines. Clan Korval is not, I think, without enemies. It must have occurred to you that your presence endangers not only the port but this entire planet."

Anger flared, though she spoke nothing but the truth. Jeeves had done what he could, given the meager infrastructure that had been in place. Certainly, there was nothing like a planetary defense net in place on Surebleak . . . one might, without exercising undue optimism, add *yet* to that statement. They had plans, and a design, but that was well outside of TerraTrade's need to know.

He took another careful breath and met Soreya Kasveini's eyes as calmly as he was able.

"Clan Korval has never been without enemies. It had long been our practice to extend such protections as we had to the port and the planet on which we were dependent. That is, after all, both good business and good husbandry."

Her gaze remained firm, and for a moment he thought she might ask further.

Self-preservation, or a simple realization that this line of questioning was . . . somewhat aside her mandate, brought a sigh to her lips, even as she glanced down and touched the button of her recorder.

"Thank you; I believe that those are all of my questions. If a need for clarity or expansion arises, I or another member of the team will stop by to speak with you again."

"I understand."

He stood when she did, and bowed.

"I appreciate your efforts," he said, "on behalf of Surebleak Port."

She returned the bow, but not the sentiment, which he supposed was fair enough. He touched the plate on his desk and the door to the anteroom opened to reveal the largeness that was Nelirikk.

"Team Leader Kasveini is leaving," Val Con told him. "Pray see her out."

* * *

The day was fine and clear, warmer here than in Surebleak city, on this little bit of land surrounded on three sides by the creamy waters of the lake. It was a large lake, and showed admirably clear in the maps left behind by the Gilmour Agency. It had no name, merely a geographic designation, though someone had taken the trouble to make a brief note: "fresh, mineral."

Near the center of the little pennisula were various markers and machineries—the tools of architects and surveyors. There were, this morning, no workers at the site, though they had been about recently, leaving behind items associated with their trades in neat piles, and sections of cleared land marked off with string and stakes.

The land toward lakeside was grassy, sloping gently down to the water. The work site was at the height of land, closer to the treeline on the mainland than the lake.

There was very little sound—a small breeze dancing through the grasses, a slight crackling where a tarp that had not been fully secured fluttered in that same breeze; the playful plash of small waves against the edges of the land.

And the sound, faint at first, but growing rapidly louder, of an engine.

A shadow moved over the tree tops, branches bent and flailed as the shadow became a aircraft, swooping in low and fast.

Three bombs and the peninsula was no more; the lake turgid with mud, as the shadow flickered over small, outraged waves, cutting hard to the left—

. . . and was gone.

* * *

Well, Val Con thought carefully, it wasn't as if the survey team leader had stated in so many words that Korval's mere presence on-world was being weighed as an on-going, and active, threat to the welfare of the port.

On the other hand, she hadn't had to; the insinuation had been more than enough.

His temper was beyond frayed. A glance at the screen showed Nelirikk alone in the anteroom, the door that opened onto port decently closed, and no one waiting for a moment of the Road Boss's attention.

Good. That was good.

He considered closing the office for an early lunch, but the thought of going into the Emerald and perhaps having to tell Pat Rin . . . No. Best simply to sit, and collect himself. A cup of tea would not be amiss, and that he could provide for himself.

Closing his eyes, he worked through a mental sequence meant to impart calm and clear thought. After the exercise was done, he sat for several more minutes, eyes closed, just . . . breathing.

Somewhat calmer, he rose, and moved to the back of the little office, stepping 'round the partition into the private area. The door to the utilitarian facilities was at the far left; quick oven, tea-maker, and cold box, grouped as a small galley, center; and the back door, or, as Miri had it, the bolt hole, at the right.

He touched the tea-maker, and waited while it brewed a cup of heavily caffeinated tea. It was a compromise beverage, preferred by neither Road Boss, but grudgingly pronounced drinkable by both. It was possible that caffeine was not precisely what his temper needed at the moment. Perhaps he ought to see if they might expand the pantry's holdings so far as mint.

The 'maker pinged, announcing the end of the brew cycle, and he drew off a cup, taking it with him back to the main office.

Carefully, he set the cup on the desk and stood by his chair, considering the song of Miri, which he heard, always, inside of his head. He detected no discord or signs of distress, which was good—one of them ought to be enjoying a calm interlude. It did, however, give rise to the question of what had occurred—or was occurring—with Emissary Twelve. If that person was indeed one of the Short Lives . . .

The bell over the port-side door rang. With emphasis. Val Con looked to the screen as Theo strode into the outer office, stopping before Nelirikk's desk, legs braced and face set.

"Is my brother in?" she snapped. "I need to talk to him."

The image of the bolt hole flashed before his mind's eye, but really, there was no choice. To turn Theo out onto the port in that face was to be an accessory to murder.

He crossed the room and opened the door to the front office.

"Good morning, Theo," he said, keeping his voice smooth and his face only pleasant. "I was just having a cup of tea. Will you join me?"

* * *

"I understand that the port's expanding," Theo said, "and that's why they needed to lay a *cantra* fine against us. But to hit us with those citations—survey team or no survey team! That's not just reading the regs with a heavy eye; it's inventing whole new paragraphs!"

Val Con was slouched at ease in his desk chair, ankle on opposite knee, tea cup cradled in his hands.

It was, Theo thought, not very good tea. Surprisingly bad, really, with 'way too much caffeine and an oily texture—more like coffee than tea. Despite which, she had a swallow, hoping to loosen her throat.

"The regs," Val Con said, apparently having decided that she'd finished saying her piece, which she guessed she had. "The regs do give the portmaster's discretion rather wide scope. Necessary, as I think you would agree, as all ports are not one port, and conditions even at sister ports may vary . . . significantly."

Theo slumped back in the visitor's chair and *fuffed* her hair out of her eyes.

"But this portmaster—"

"Portmaster Liu, as all of us, very much wishes for TerraTrade to find Surebleak Port worthy of an upgraded certification. The survey team has many reasons to find for us—there are not so many full-service ports in this sector."

"There isn't any *trade* in this sector," Theo pointed out.

"No; you are harsh. There is some small amount of trade and traffic in the sector, and the presence of a certified port can do nothing but increase trade. Which is an attractive proposition to TerraTrade."

He sipped his tea, carefully, Theo thought.

"However, it does not benefit TerraTrade, which is to say, it does not benefit *trade* to certify an unworthy port. Above all, the process by which ratings and upgrades are determined must be beyond reproach. If the portmaster on a given port is known to read the regs with a heavy eye, as you have it, that is acceptable. A lax portmaster on a port which will, appropriately rated, become the primary draw to trade in the sector—that endangers the process, and TerraTrade's *melant'i*, as well as Surebleak's chances for an upgrade. So Portmaster Liu has reasoned—and I think she is correct."

Theo shook her head.

"She said she came down *particularly* hard on *Bechimo* because I'm your sister. That's not running a tight port, that's reading the regs out of one eye for me and the other eye for everybody else."

"Ah. Do you have evidence that she has imposed lesser sanctions on other ships which have compromised the shipping lanes?" Val Con asked interestedly.

Theo frowned at him.

"Where would I find evidence?"

"The portmaster's log, naturally," he said, mildly. "We might easily find if you are the first, and a warning to others—or if you have been shamefully mistreated solely because you are my sister."

He raised his voice.

"Nelirikk, would you please send the current portmaster's log to my screen?"

"Yes," came the answer over the intercom.

Val Con extended an arm and turned the portable screen toward her.

"Please," he said, rising with effortless grace. "My resources are your resources. Will you like more tea?"

"No, thank you," she managed, and added. "What is the blend? So I know to avoid it."

It was honest, but it wasn't polite, and Theo bit the inside of her cheek.

Inner calm, she told herself, biting hard, and raised her eyes to Val Con's face, expecting at the least a cool glance, and an upraised eyebrow.

But Val Con was laughing.

"I shall make you a gift of the tin, so that you may always have it before you as an example."

"No, I—"

She took a deep breath.

"I'm sorry," she said.

"Sorry? For being Father's daughter, and a member of this family?" He shook his head, grin lingering. "Allow me to compliment you, Theo. That was perfectly done."

She glared at him.

"Why're you drinking it, if you don't like it?"

"It is a compromise. Here, let me clear these away so that you may have room to work. A moment . . ."

He vanished 'round the partition in the back of the office, boots making no sound at all on the plastic floor. Theo adjusted the screen and entered her search terms.

#

The log showed that Master Liu ran a balanced and reasonable port—or at least she had for the last half-year, local. It would be interesting, Theo thought, to do a compare and contrast of port conditions and penalties before Korval had settled on Surebleak and after.

It would also take some time, and she was on a borrowed computer.

Bechimo, she said in bond-space.

There was no answer, though she thought she'd felt the barest brush of attention.

Right. She was being censured. She sighed. Another thing to fix, but—

"Has your search yielded evidence?" Val Con asked from too near at hand.

She shook her head and looked up.

"Nothing in the last half-year. Probably nothing at all, though to be thorough, I'd have to read the whole log, since Korval arrived on planet."

"Ah." He looked politely interested. "And will you do so?"

"In my spare time," she told him; "when I have access to my own computer."

"As you will." He placed a tea tin on the edge of the desk, and sat down in his chair. She turned the screen back to him, eyes on the tin.

"*Bitter Truth*?" she asked, feeling her eyebrows rise. "Who names a tea *Bitter Truth*?"

"Obviously, the White Wing Beverage Company does, though in earnest or in jest, I dare not speculate."

He paused to glance at the screen, then turned a serious look in her direction.

"I wonder, Theo, if you wish to . . . emancipate yourself, so that you might establish your own family, or corporation. As you point out, being known as Korval kin is not necessarily advantageous, and in fact has been dangerous for you and for your ship."

She stared at him. *Emancipate* herself? Repudiate Father, and Luken, Miri, and, well—Val Con? Even Lady Kareen was—

"Um, no," she said carefully, to her brother's speculative green gaze; "I don't want to divorce myself from the—*our*—family." She sighed. "I just wish you were a little less prone to trouble!"

He grinned.

"One might return the compliment, were it not well-known in the family that we are, as individuals and as a unit, prone to trouble."

She felt her mouth soften, and gave him a nod.

"Point. But, even if I did start my own family, and formally divorce myself from Clan Korval, I don't think the people who've been hunting *Bechimo* are going to see—or care about—that level of detail."

"They do seem to find the fine print a challenge," Val Con agreed. "And here we approach my topic. As you are yourself kin without being clan, it may have escaped your attention that Clan Korval is a very small . . . family, indeed. Dangerously small, one might say. For our own security, we need to improve our situation. The choices before us are to disband, and allow each member to form their own alliances with other families or clans—or we might merge with another small clan and thus form a larger, to the benefit of both."

He gave her a wise look.

"However, as we have just discussed, Clan Korval's marriage portion will inevitably include trouble; and there are not many clans—of any size—who seek to add to their stores of trouble. As we are now placed on Surebleak, and as Surebleak will, sooner rather than later, so I believe, evolve a hybrid culture, Miri has proposed a third solution, which looks toward the future, rather than seeking to accommodate the past."

He paused, head tipped to one side.

"I wonder if this might not be better discussed over an early lunch at the Emerald. If you have time, of—"

"Scout, attention," Nelirikk's big voice came over the intercom. "Status reports incoming. There have been explosions on several streets in the city, moving in toward the port. Jeeves—"

The bell over the front door shrieked and clanged as it burst off its hanger. In the screen, the port-side door burst open, admitting one man, weapon ready. Neilirikk surged to his feet; There came the sound of pellet fire, and a second figure, throwing a smoking—

An alarm went off, wailing like a sackful of cats in a fight to the death.

Theo was on her feet, turning toward the door—and was jerked to a stop by Val Con's hand around her wrist.

"This way!" he snapped, and pulled her with him toward the back of the office.

#

They emerged into a thin, smelly alley. Val Con glanced over his shoulder, and let go of her wrist.

"Stay near," he murmured, and moved, silent as a shadow, to the right, down-port.

Theo followed, astonished to find that she still held the stupid tea tin. She thought about dropping it, then didn't. No reason making it easy for them, if they got through Nelirikk and out the back door.

It didn't, she thought, look like the alley had much use. From her mental map of the port, she thought they were heading to the Emerald. Given Pat Rin and the whole rest of the family, they could probably seal the Emerald up into a fortress if they needed to, and—

"Theo," *Bechimo* said inside of bond-space. "There is a group of armed individuals waiting around the corner your brother is approaching. Hold back, let him distract them, then run. I will guide you to safety—"

Theo increased her stride, and was very nearly on Val Con's heels as he stepped 'round the corner . . .

A heavy, meaty sound, followed by a grunt—that was what she heard before she leapt around the corner, going wide, so she didn't crowd Val Con, or trip over him if the sound had been him going down . . .

One stranger in leathers was on the ground, and Val Con was dancing under a blow from a second leathered person when Theo joined the fray.

"There she is!" somebody shouted, and Theo was dancing and ducking herself, turning hard on a heel and kicking backward, hearing a kneecap crunch.

"Theo!" *Bechimo* wailed. "Save yourself!"

"And leave my brother?" she demanded, before her attention was grabbed by another thug, swinging down hard, like he meant to flatten her. She ducked under the descending fist, opened the tin, and threw the contents into face and eyes, eliciting a satisfying yelp, even as she kicked another assailant.

Val Con, she saw in a frenzied glimpse, was holding his own, having knocked down another opponent.

It was an ugly fight; though nobody, thank the gods, was risking a gun. There were too many bodies in the thin alley, and the only way to go on was to go through. Six to two, Theo calculated, but two of them were down already—

"Behind you!" screamed *Bechimo*, and she hit the ground, rolling, hearing something strike the 'crete with shattering force.

A boot came out of nowhere, aimed at her head. She kept rolling, and grabbed the braced leg, taking him down, half on top of her. She kneed him, pushed him off, and managed to snap to her feet. She was on the outside of the fight, she saw, with three assailants concentrating on Val Con, though one was hanging back.

She saw something gleam in that one's hand, and lunged forward, thinking *knife* even as a pop sounded, and the alley began to fill with acrid-tasting smoke. Theo coughed, backing away. The assailant with the canister dropped it and turned, kicking hard and fast, connecting with her knee. Agony flared, but she kept her feet, swinging—blinded by tears, and the alley was swimming out of focus, bordered in black.

Something struck her in the right side; she gasped, her lungs clogged with smoke.

* * *

Lisle raised the butt of her gun again, then held back. The skinny blondie was down and out, crumpled up small on the sticky alley floor.

She turned in time to see Benny and Jake rush the guy, who was still fighting, despite the gas, and despite the fact that his right arm was hanging limp. She raised the gun—and thrust it in its holster, as the security siren wailed toward them.

"Leave him!" she yelled, reaching down and hauling the unconscious woman up over her shoulder in a rough carry. "We got her, that's good enough!"

Benny got in one more kick at the guy's head—not a solid blow—and the three of them were running, leaving their fallen to the mercy of the gas.

Behind them, the guy rallied, straightened, and threw, the knife flying true, as the thrower slid down the wall and collapsed.

Chapter Six

Surebleak
Jelaza Kazone

"Shields up full!"

Jeeves's voice rang across the garden, as the sky dimmed perceptibly.

"Damage report!"

Miri was on her feet, the brown cat cuddled against her breast. Daav and Aelliana were up, too; Emissary Twelve lay like the dead.

"yos'Galan's land has been bombed," Jeeves stated. "Damage to supplies and terrain. Defensive resources are low, but I have deployed what is possible."

"Casualties?" Miri demanded, stomach tightening.

"Day crew had not yet arrived. Work suspended until further notice."

"Anything else?"

"Boss Sherton reports old borer and earth-moving equipment on the move toward a village nominally under her protection. The settlement is being evacuated. Joyita has hacked the command lines; *Bechimo* is building stop-codes. The goal is to preserve homesteads and crops."

"ID on hostiles?"

"Joyita is working on a match. He reports negative on Scout vessels, as well as the light-ships utilized by the Department of the Interior. Status report: Localized shields have been activated at prime locations in the city. Shelter-in-place has been transmitted.

The portmaster's office has been alerted to the presence of hostile craft--"

Val Con.

Miri reached; found him at the end of her mental fingers, more or less calm, though somewhat weary.

She blinked back into the garden.

Daav was looking grim, Aelliana only slightly less so.

"Seems like somebody's committed," Miri said, and shivered. They'd been waiting for this, or something like it. For the DOI to finally realize that Korval was as vulnerable as it would ever be, *right now*, and decide to throw everything they had, *right now*, at Surebleak.

"They have not attacked the house," Aelliana said. "Surely that would be the first priority."

Miri shook her head.

"They'll figure the house is base, and well-defended. They'll take less-defended targets first, so they won't have any surprises at their back when they turn their full attention here."

"They're striking on many fronts at once in order to confuse," Daav murmured.

"That, too."

"Status report," Jeeves stated. "*Bechimo's* codes have been transmitted; the machinery has stopped advancing. Civilian evacuation continues, but a human tech crew is being dispatched to the machines."

There was a movement at the edge of her eye. Miri looked down in time to see Emissary Twelve raise her arms, and roll to her feet with a speed and grace not to be found among the ordinary run of Clutch.

Emissary Twelve turned to face Miri; the cat she was still cuddling hissed, claws pricking skin through her sweater.

"I have been the recipient of offensive action," Emissary Twelve stated. "Who dares strike the emissary of the Elders?"

"Knock it off," Miri muttered. Gods knew what would happen if she put the cat down; probably it would attack, and Emissary Twelve would declare war on feline-kind.

"Korval," a rough voice said softly. "May I relieve you of your burden?"

Right.

With a sense of relief all out of proportion with the problem, Miri handed the cat to Daav, and turned back to Emissary Twelve, deliberately reaching for the High Tongue.

"You were inadvertently struck down while receiving the Elder Tree's explanation of events, which you had requested. Apparently, the flow of information from the Tree overcame your sensibilities and you fainted."

There; let her get snippy about Ren Zel again.

"I do not faint," Emissary Twelve stated.

"Every event is unique, the first time it happens."

"Status report!" Jeeves announced.

"Shops on six streets are on fire; emergency crews and the patrol have been called out. Gas canisters have exploded at the entrances to the Portmaster's office, Andy Mack's repair shop, the Emerald Casino, Tantara Floor Coverings, and the office of the Road Boss."

Miri didn't have to reach this time; she was *there*, inside his head, staring at the screen with him: Men bursting into the outer office, Nelirikk rising like a mountain out of a cloud bank, Theo spinning--

They jumped with one will, and were on the way to the bolt hole, dragging Theo by the wrist.

The alley stank of nothing but its usual mold and mud; she let Theo go with a muttered *stay close*, and moved cautiously toward the corner. She could hear boot soles moving on grit, heavy breathing, the whisper of leather against leather . . .

Six, she estimated; waiting for them. She glanced over her shoulder at Theo, keeping slightly back, ready on the balls of her feet, eyes intent. Right then, Miri thought--we go first.

She moved, fast, snaking 'round the corner, dodging a fist, and landing a kick. The first was down, as she swung to face—

Something hit her square between the shoulder blades. Her sight went black, and she yelled, crashing to her knees on grass--*grass*. A breeze supported her like a comrade's arm around her waist, and she blinked the Tree Court into reality.

"Jeeves! Port Security to the utility alley behind the Road Boss's office, now! Val Con, Theo--six attackers. In the office, Nelirikk's down."

"Working," Jeeves said.

She lurched upward, and for a heartbeat she saw the alley again, ghostly and grey--stumbled, and felt her shoulders caught in a strong grip, while the breeze pushed her upright.

"Miri!" Aelliana snapped.

She blinked again, staring into bright green eyes.

"Threw me outta his head. Helluva time to learn that trick."

She shook her head.

"I gotta get down there."

Aelliana's fingers tightened on her shoulders.

"Your place is here, Korval," she said, the High Tongue ringing like crystal bells in the quiet garden. "You have given your orders. Allow those who serve you to act."

She swallowed, tasting smoke.

Delm-for-the-day, Robertson.

Her laugh morphed into a cry as the kick landed, slamming her back into the wall, her right arm going with an audible snap.

Aelliana braced her, guiding her collapse until she was again kneeling in the grass.

"*Van'chela*, of your grace."

"Yes," said Daav. "One burden for another, Pilot."

He put the brown cat on Aelliana's shoulder on his way past, and the next moment, Miri felt herself swung up into strong arms.

"I can walk," she said, her voice so unsteady she didn't even believe herself.

"Of course you can," Daav said, moving briskly toward the pathway. "Merely, at the moment, I can walk better."

* * *

Emissary Twelve watched the three humans, with attendant predators, depart. The delm of Korval had fallen ill, and the others had an imperative to care for and guard her. This was comprehensible.

In the throes of this crisis, they had forgotten the emissary of the Elders. This was less comprehensible, but possibly the humans did not understand the Elders well enough to know that one removed one's attention from them at one's very great peril.

This could also be said of Emissary Twelve, under most of the circumstances into which she might have been quickened. That she had been called forth to perform diplomacy, considerably lessened the peril the humans might expect to confront on her account. She might yet need to resort to force in order to obtain what the Elders had ordered her to bring to them, but--not yet.

This naive forgetfulness, in fact, served the purpose of the Elders, Emissary Twelve thought. She now had the opportunity to question the Elder Tree in her own way, without the interference of the delm of Korval.

They would see, now, who prevailed, when it came to strength against strength.

She turned toward the Tree—and paused, tantalized.

An . . . aroma reached her nose. A delicious and provocative scent that awoke feelings of a strange and particular hunger.

She knelt down, scanning the ground, looking for the source of that wonderful –

There!

A round object lying among the grasses, green and definitely organic, yet seeming to glow, as if lit from within.

Emissary Twelve extended a three-fingered hand. The object fairly leapt into her palm. The scent was stronger, more seductive . . . compelling. She *must* eat of this fruit, whatever it was, or she would never be free of hunger again.

Fruit did not behave in this manner, so her store of memories informed her.

Fruit did not behave in this manner.

But traps did.

She brought her hand up to throw the thing away from her--and stopped, hand falling, as hunger spiked. A peculiar hunger; not merely a need to replenish her resources, but a hunger specific to the fruit itself.

The skin of her palm was warming gently, agreeably.

She looked down to find that the fruit had obligingly fallen into quarters. The Elders and the mission she had been born to fell before the assault of the fruit's promise, and faded into nothing.

Emissary Twelve picked up one single quarter and brought it to her mouth.

* * *

Miri roused, and sat up, grabbing for her hideaway, even as she realized that this was no back alley, but the morning parlor, and she was lying, not on sticky, cracked crete, but on the window seat.

She sighed, and slid the gun away. Aelliana, who was watching her interestedly from a chair set at a prudent distance, gave her a smile.

"As you bore no wounds, and your arm is perfectly unbroken, we decided against the 'doc," she said. "Would you care for a cup of tea?"

"Not just yet, thanks." Miri looked 'round the room, seeing Daav sitting, just to the left and behind Aelliana. He had a brown cat on his shoulder and a white cat on his knee.

"Where's Emissary Twelve?" Miri asked sharply.

Aelliana got to her feet.

"She is in the Tree Court. Jeeves—"

"All hands on deck!" Joyita's voice rang out.

"Repeat! All hands on deck! The captain has been abducted!"

* * *

In the Southern Suite, Clarence swore, got to his feet and grabbed his jacket.

He was out the door and running for the staircase before the second call was completed. At that, he wasn't the quickest of them; Win Ton was well ahead. Kara, on Clarence's very heels, saw him pelting down the stairs, taking two and three at a time, silent as a ghost--to be overtaken and left behind by an orange-and-grey flash.

"Hevelin!" Kara cried.

Clarence threw her a grin over his shoulder.

"Bet he's in my chair when we get aboard!"

* * *

"Abducted!" Chernak repeated, coming to her feet. "Who would dare?"

Stost was already on his way to the door.

"Halt!" shouted Diglon Rifle.

"Commander Relgen and her second-in-command are coming here to interview you, in order to best determine your future lives."

Chernak turned to him.

"Our captain has been abducted. All hands are called to the ship. You heard this."

Diglon considered her.

"Do you say it? *Your captain?*"

"What else should we say?" Stost demanded from the doorway.

Diglon raised his fist in a salute between comrades.

"If that is what you say, Pathfinders--then, go! Duty calls, and glory awaits!"

"With such a captain and such a ship, it could hardly be otherwise," Chernak answered. She returned the salute, and spun, running after Stost, through the door.

They were gone, then, and Diglon, alone in the ready room, allowed himself to grin.

"Jeeves," he said; "please be sure that nothing impedes the Pathfinders on the way to their ship."

Chapter Seven

Surebleak
Jelaza Kazone

"Who?" Miri demanded, pushing back from the desk, and directing her comments toward the ceiling. "These—" she waved a scornful hand at the screen—"these're the hired help. What we need to know is who paid 'em!"

"Working," Jeeves said, sounding particularly machine-like, which she guessed she'd bought and paid for. Wasn't any kind of good sense to yell at your info-source while he was working—or when he gave you info you didn't like, either. Data was data, but, still—

"I know you're working," she said. "I'm in a temper 'cause there's nothing for me to be working on."

"Understood," Jeeves said, his voice warm—even sympathetic.

Miri got up and walked over to the window. She stood there, hands behind her back, staring out at the inner garden and Jelaza Kazone's enormous trunk. Daav and Aelliana were in the Tree Court, though she couldn't see them from this window. Jeeves had reported Emissary Twelve in a *trance or coma*, her palms flat against the Tree, and Miri'd sent them to cope, once she came to.

"Just don't let her remove you from Surebleak," she said.

"Korval," Daav had responded, with a formal bow. "We shall contrive."

"That's what I'm afraid of," she'd told him, and waved the pair of them off.

99

Now, she sighed, and closed her eyes, reviewing the mental Rainbow exercise, to achieve calmness and distance.

The colors spun behind her eyes; she took a deep breath, and sighed it out.

As bad as the news was from all over, she thought; it could have been worse. Much worse. It looked like a planned attempt to have lots of little things going bad all over—out back of Melina Sherton's turf; Shan's peninsula; in the city; on the port—sowing confusion and dismay, like Luken would have it, though he was usually talking in the context of card games. That was good tactics. And to a degree, confusion and dismay had been sown.

They had a handle on what had happened where—in the city, windows had been broken, small fires started, loud arguments erupted spontaneously, drawing shopkeepers out on the sidewalks, so that the third partner could slip in and perform petty theft . . .

On the port, gas had been deployed at the main entrances of the Emerald Casino, the Portmaster's office, Tantara Floor Coverings, Andy Mack's repair shop.

The Road Boss's office was unique in hosting an actual enemy action involving sleepy gas, and guns. Not a good combination, and Miri was inclined to think that it hadn't worked quite according to plan.

One of the invaders through the front door had been killed by Nelirikk, who didn't go down quite as fast as he would have, had he been Val Con's size. He'd gotten two shots off—killed one, maybe winged the other, or maybe just convinced her to run away.

Nelirikk himself had taken a hit, besides getting his lungs full of sleepy gas. He'd been taken to the Port Trauma Center and placed in an autodoc. According to papers found on the body, the deader was Malapat See, first mate on the small cargo ship *Zindel*.

Val Con and Theo had managed to get out the back door, and here was where the story turned scary . . . Val Con was also in a 'doc at the Port Trauma Center; the three deaders all carrying papers identifying them as crew on *Teramondi*, out of Waymart. Naturally.

Theo was, according to *Bechimo*—and who was she to doubt a ship on the matter of the whereabouts of his captain?—Theo was located on that same *Teramondi*, against her will. So *Bechimo* insisted, and she wasn't going to argue that point, either.

The port was locked down, which was good, as far as it went. A determined captain—or a crazy one—could lift despite the niceties; she might even be able to dodge whatever weapons the port could bring to bear. But if she didn't dodge with skill and luck, her ship was dead—and so was Theo.

So far, *Teramondi* was playing nice, which made sense. If she was a hostage, then Theo was the captain's payday, and no reason to put her in harm's way.

Miri turned away from the window, walked back to the desk, and frowned down at the screen.

Penn had ID'd a couple slackers from his streets, and had sent a vid of their questioning. Miri scooped Fondi off the chair and sat down, putting him on her lap. He jumped down, naturally enough, and she leaned forward to tap up the vid.

The two slackers were Jewlz Abnety—tall, ruddy, and balding—and Peet Forsh—short, with unkempt dark hair and a scraggly beard.

They cheerfully admitted to taking money to do mischief.

"Why wouldn't we?" asked Jewlz, with a shrug. "Just bidness, Penn. Can't blame us for doin' bidness."

"Dunno," Peet said, shaking his head over the question of who exactly had hired them. "Never seen 'er before, and no, we din't ask who she was. Lady wants us to have 'er name, she'll offer, right? Figured 'er for a newbie, but what's to worry. 'er money was good."

It turned out her money *had* been good—plain and serviceable Sureleak cash, which they took out of their pockets and put down on the desk with visible reluctance.

"C'mon, now, Penn, we earned that cash," Jewlz said; "an' it ain't likely we're gonna get the rest, now you decided to butt in."

"That's not all of it?" Penn asked, eyeing the considerable sum they'd dug out of their pockets.

Peet threw his partner a frown.

"Nah, ain't all of it," he told Penn, sounding aggrieved. "Half up front; half after we done the job. S'posed to meet 'er at Jimstin's hour gone. Were on our way over there when the sleet-eatin' patrol picked us up, and dragged us over here to you, like you din't know who we was! All us growed up t'gether, right here on these streets, din't we?"

"That's right," Penn said. "I figured you two would know what going on. Always got your ears on the street. I know that."

Peet actually looked mollified.

"Anyhoots," he said with a shrug, "prolly there's no payday, now we're so late."

He was, Miri thought, probably right about that.

"Maybe, maybe not," Penn said. "Tell you what. You pick up what's already been paid, and go along with Joey here, and his friend Kyan from the patrol."

Peet and Jewlz exchanged a look. A very wary look, for which Miri didn't exactly blame them. They both looked over their shoulders at Joey Valish, Penn's head 'hand, who was keeping an eye on things from the rear. Joey gave them an easy nod.

"Go where?" Jewlz asked, turning back to Penn.

"Just step down to Jimstin's. Could be the lady waited for you. If so, I'd like a word with her, that's all."

Peet's face rumpled behind the beard.

"Ah, c'mon, Penn! You're gonna blow our cred! How're we gonna do bidness, after rattin' a customer?"

Penn considered him.

"Might be you'll hafta find some bidness other than wrecking my streets," he said mildly, and Miri saw Jewlz take a step back from the desk.

"But, sleet, have it your way," Penn continued, still in that too-mild voice. "We grew together on these streets, like you said. So maybe you'd like to leave that money right here, and step along with Patrol Officer Kyan to the Whosegow, an' keep your cred."

"Hey!" yelled Peet.

"Or, you can keep the money and take Joey and Kyan with you down to Jimstin's and point out the lady, if it so happens she's there."

Peet looked at Jewlz.

Jewlz looked at Peet.

They both looked at the money.

"Thunder an' ice," Jewlz muttered.

"Yeah, yeah." Peet leaned forward and grabbed a handful of money, shoving it into his coat pocket.

"So, Joey, you gonna buy us a drink?"

"Figured you two'd stand me," Joey answered. "Bein' as you just had a payday."

Jewlz finished stashing his money, and nodded at Penn.

"Good luck, *Boss*," he said, and the look on his face was downright ugly, Miri thought.

Joey might've had the same issue with the tone of voice. He looked over Jewlz's head to Penn, who moved his right shoulder in a shrug so slight it took somebody used to dealing with Liadens to see it.

"C'mon, you two!" Joey said, nice and loud. "I got a bad thirst comin' on, just listenin' to the pair o'you. Let's pick up Kyan and hit Jimston's, what say?"

"Sounds great," Peet muttered, as him and Jewlz followed Joey out.

Penn stood up from behind his desk, and the vid ended.

Miri sighed. No doubt but Peet was right; the newbie lady'd gotten off the street well before trouble started, and was intending to stay low, if she hadn't left planet by now.

Granting Penn had dibs, Miri wanted a word with the lady, herself.

"Not much chance of that, either," she muttered, shaking her head. She raised her voice slightly.

"Port's on lock-down," she said.

"Yes, Miri," said Jeeves.

"Right, but here's what—she didn't have to come down at Port. Could've taken a rough landing back in the beyond, past Melina's boundaries, so she could get out fast."

"*Bechimo* and I have been analyzing traffic, with just such a scenario in mind," Jeeves told her. "Thus far, we have not found evidence of any unauthorized lifts. Nor have we found evidence of any ship, saving *Bechimo*, landing in districts other than Surebleak Port, going back six local months."

Which, Miri thought grumpily, could just mean that the shielding on Ms. Newbie's ship was that good. On the other hand, she could be one of the several agents of the Department of the Interior they knew to be lurking in Surebleak's population.

Or she could not be a newbie at all, but a 'bleaker from another turf, who happened to be a member of Take Back Surebleak, and wanted to stir things up.

Trouble with you, Robertson, she told herself, is you married into trouble, and the list of people unhappy with Clan Korval and its doings just keeps getting longer.

She sighed and moved over to the buffet to draw herself a cup of coffee.

The dust-up in the city, now, that did look like Take Back Surebleak. Knocking out windows and setting fire to small business—that was a page, or even two, out of the former Bosses handbook on how to intimidate streeters.

On the port, though . . .

On the port, they'd hit the Portmaster's office, and the Emerald—owned and operated by Boss Conrad, the conqueror of Surebleak, himself. Luken bel'Tarda's Tantara Floor Coverings displayed the Tree-and-Dragon right in the front window—the same front window that'd been knocked out. Andy Mack, who'd been on Surebleak the whole time was a vocal supporter of the changes, the Council of Bosses, and the new ordering of everything.

And the Road Boss . . .

The Road Boss hadn't exactly made themselves the friends of the streeter on the street. First problem was that they followed the rules and regulations put down by the Council of Bosses; imposed and collected fines for improper use of the Road, and weight limit violations.

Not only that, they didn't sell exceptions to those who were willing to pay up to half the cost of a legitimate fine as a bribe for the Road Boss to look the other way. Worse, they'd done nothing more or less than made a zample of the used-to-was chairman of the Citizens Heavy Loads Committee, for trying to get the exceptions gig working like it was BBC—Before Boss Conrad.

Sure, Take Back Surebleak had a grievance against the Road Boss.

But, Miri thought, sipping her coffee, did they have a grievance big enough to justify taking a hostage? The Old Bosses hadn't done much in the way of hostage-taking—more efficient to kill trouble-makers, or burn 'em out.

Add in the hiring of off-worlders to do the street's dirty work—it just didn't scan like Surebleak.

The Department of the Interior, now: hostages and mind-games was their home turf. If it was the Department, the the next thing they could expect would be an offer to trade—Theo for Val Con, and Val Con knowing just a little too exactly what they'd likely do to Theo if he refused the deal.

"Courier at the gate," Jeeves said; making some effort to keep his voice soft. She jumped anyway, and spilled her coffee.

By the time she had mopped up, the front door bell had rung, and Jeeves reported Mr. pel'Kana going to answer.

She stepped to the desk to watch the live feed.

Mr. pel'Kana opened the door to a Surebleak kid ID'd on the screen as Jilanne Alami. She handed him a bag.

"Customer said it's for the delm of Korval, but if the Road Boss was to home, that would be OK, too."

"Thank you," Mr. pel'Kana said solemnly, and put a couple bits into the kid's hand.

"Thanks!" she responded, and swung onto the back of a bright red duocycle, of the sort that were showing up everywhere all of a sudden. Miri blamed the Scouts.

She executed a showy turn, nearly putting the cycle flat down on its side, and zoomed off for the gate.

Mr. pel'Kana closed the front door; the screen flipped back to the news queue. Miri put her coffee cup down on the desk, and there was a knock at the office door.

"Come," she said, and Mr. pel'Kana and the bag entered.

"This arrived by courier, your Ladyship," he said. "For the delm of Korval or the Road Boss."

"Thank you, Mr. pel'Kana." The bag was heavier than it looked, and Miri felt a shiver go down her spine.

"Would you care for a tray, ma'am? Mrs. ana'Tak has just taken some sweet rolls out."

"Thank you, but no," Miri said; and Mr. pel'Kana bowed and went away, closing the door quietly behind him.

Miri carried the bag to the desk and opened it.

Black space leather unrolled across desktop and keyboard. She didn't need to see anything more than the pattern of wear on the left sleeve to know whose jacket it was.

Even knowing already that Theo had been taken, and exactly where she was being held, it took her breath to see the Jump pilot's jacket that Theo would part with only at the cost of her life.

Deep breath, Robertson, she told herself.

She put her hands on the leather—well-worn, supple as silk—and methodically went through each and every pocket, no matter how secret, putting what she found in each on the desk.

When she was done, she had a tidy little pile—three cantra pieces; a lesser amount of Terran cash; a sleek little hideaway; a multiuse tool; a snap-knife; a GPS; a data-key with probably her PIC and guild info on it . . .

Exactly the sort of things you expect to find in the pockets of working pilot, except for one thing.

Pilot's license.

Miri searched again, making sure of all the pockets, public and private.

No, whoever had taken Theo had kept the license, too, and that definitively took this part of today's business off Surebleak, and put it into DOI territory.

Funny, she thought, looking down at the jacket, and the little pile of Theo's belongings—funny, there wasn't any note. Or maybe not, given her reaction to the jacket's arrival. Maybe they were meant to stew for a while, softened up by worry, before the DOI made its proposal.

Miri took another deep breath, closed her eyes, and ran the Scout's Rainbow, seeking calm, and distance.

"Jeeves," she said, when she was done; "what's the update with Emissary Twelve?"

"She remains in communion with the Tree."

"Got a lot of catching up to do," Miri said. "Aelliana and Daav?"

"They are following local events via hand-held."

Miri nodded.

"Ask Mr. pel'Kana to take them a tray, please. I—"

She put her hand on Theo's jacket; looked at the things she had taken from the pockets—and the one thing that she hadn't.

"I'm going to take a nap. Please see that no one disturbs me for the next hour."

There was a small pause, as if she'd startled him, which, she might've done, at that. Peculiar time for a nap, somebody might think.

In most cases, it would be true.

In this case, she needed to talk to a man about a jacket—a man who was currently in an autodoc at the Port.

Chapter Eight

"Theo."

Barely more than a whisper, almost too soft to hear, but it sent a shiver of pain through her head; light flared, and she stopped hearing anything.

. . .

"Theo, please."

The voice again; still soft, but with an edge to it, maybe panic. She tried to reach out to it—the voice. Tried to say, "Hey, calm—"

Pain flickered, hot, like lightning inside her head, followed by blackness.

. . .

"Theo, you must attend me."

Right, the voice. She remembered the voice. Not sounding so panicky, now. Determined, maybe. No, grim.

Grim, Theo thought. Grim wasn't good. In fact, grim was right on the edge of being bad.

"Theo?"

"Hold on," she said—or at least she meant to say it. She had the idea that she hadn't done much in the way of vocalizing.

Regardless, the voice heard her.

"Theo, what is your condition?"

Her *condition*? She thought. Pain flickered, and she breathed into it, like she'd taken a solid strike while dancing *menfri'at*—and she remembered: The bullies breaking into the Road Boss's office, Nelirikk roaring to his feet, the screen full of smoke, Val Con dragging her out the back door with him, into the alley, the corner where the *other* bullies had been waiting, *Bechimo* urging her to run—

"*Bechimo*?" she thought then, and felt bond-space open around her.

"Yes. You should have run."

"No," she managed. "No, that would've—where's Val Con?"

There was a flicker of lightning, distant; it hardly hurt at all.

"Theo, please, you must not risk another seizure. We have formulated a plan, but it—"

But memory was still unscrolling, implacable, unstoppable. She saw him up against the wall, three guys on him and blood on his face—

"*Where is my brother?*" Theo interrupted—calmly, considering.

Bechimo seemed to hesitate, or maybe she'd just put him off his stride.

"Your brother is safe," he said. "You are at risk. We have formulated a plan to remove you from your current situation, but it requires your active participation. What is your condition?"

Second time he'd asked for her condition, which was—odd. If they were in bond-space, he ought to *know* her condition.

"Yes," he said, answering her thought. "The key informs me of your physical condition. You have two broken ribs, and your right knee has been injured. Also, you have sustained numerous of what Clarence assures me are *minor* injuries—"

He didn't, Theo thought, sound like he agreed with Clarence's assessment.

"Clarence," *Bechimo* said stiffly, "informs me that it takes more than scraped knuckles and some bruises to slow down Daav yos'Phelium's daughter. A pair of broken ribs, says Clarence, is nothing more than a very minor inconvenience."

There was the distinct impression of a sniff—so much, Theo thought, for *Clarence's* opinion.

"At least he seems to think the knee injury's a problem," she said, mildly.

"If you are obliged to run, he agrees that it might impede you." There was a short pause.

"What I need to know is how you are held," *Bechimo* said after a moment. "Are you restrained? If so, how?"

"Don't tell me Joyita hasn't been able to get into the local systems?"

"He made an attempt and withdrew after identifying the intruder alerts, and security protocols. As you are being held on a ship, we did not wish to do anything that would cause your captors to panic and lift.

"However, if you had succumbed to another seizure, Joyita would have taken the risk, and we would have implemented the plan immediately."

"What plan?" she asked.

"The plan that the Pathfinders put together in order to win you free of your captivity, a state in which you yet reside. Theo—*what is your condition?*"

"Hold on," she murmured, concentrating on listening. She heard air whispering through a vent, and some distant pings, which might've been a ship's system working. As far as she could tell, there wasn't anyone nearby, but they probably had a camera on her. She kept her eyes closed, and took a more personal inventory.

She was lying on her back on a giving, if not exactly soft, surface—a Jump couch, she thought, identifying the tightness across her torso and thighs as webbing. Her hands were at her sides and she felt straps around the wrists, which wasn't standard for webbing in for Jump. Her chest hurt.

Actually, now that she was paying attention, she realized that most of her hurt.

"Information received," *Bechimo* said, in the flat, almost machine-like voice he used when he was really upset. "The Pathfinders will reformulate their plan."

"Wait," Theo said. "What plan?"

"The plan to liberate you," *Bechimo* said, starting to sound irritable.

"But I'm still on Surebleak Port, right? Call the Portmaster, and give her your evidence. She'll lock the ship down, send Port Security..."

"The ship on which you being held, injured and against your will," *Bechimo* interrupted tightly, "is on its fifth name. The captain is not a member of the pilot's guild. While on the face of it her license is legitimate; Joyita's research indicates that it is...irregular. Both ship and captain are for hire, and the captain does not appear to care much for laws, ownership, or local port prohibitions against smuggling. Furthermore, she was one of those who ambushed you—and your brother. If the Portmaster shows any attention to that ship, Theo, the captain could decide it is in her best interest to kill you."

"Not that likely, is it?" she asked. "She went to a lot of trouble to grab me—and she lost crew. I'm pretty sure Val Con killed the first guy..."

...and she had most likely accounted for another, she thought.

Theo took a careful breath, wincing when something grabbed in her chest and side. Right. Cracked ribs.

"Do not harm yourself," *Bechimo* said sharply.

"Just trying to assess," she said. "So, the captain's a smuggler, and she does her own close-in work. Fine. What's she want with me?"

"Joyita and Win Ton are doing research. What we suppose is that you are a hostage, to prevent Boss Conrad, Clan Korval, and by extension, the Port from taking action against captain and ship."

"But—that doesn't make any sense. Smuggler's want to work quiet, don't they? They're only calling attention to themselves by taking a hostage."

"Clarence shares your objection," *Bechimo* admitted, "though he does say that we cannot discount the possibility that the captain has, in his words, smoked out what passed for her brains. In which case, she is even more dangerous to you."

"Right. Has she made any demands?"

"Not as yet. She may be—"

"Wait," said Theo. "The door—"

"No sense pretendin' to be asleep, Blondie," a man's voice said loudly. "Monitors say you're awake."

Theo opened her eyes. The man looked vaguely familiar. She thought he might be the guy who'd tried to smash her head open. He also looked like he'd landed on his face when she tackled him—there was gravel burn down his right cheek, his lip was split,and his eyes were red.

"So," she said, her voice gritty in a raw throat, "I'm awake. What now?"

"Now?" He grinned. "*Now*, Cap'n Lisle wants a word."

* * *

There had been pain; Val Con recalled that, distantly. At the moment, however, there was no pain, only a pretty pastel fog upon which he observed himself reclining, seemingly entranced, and really quite pale and worn-looking, poor child. Doubtless, the rest would be beneficial; but in the meanwhile, he—the *he* of him—was . . . bored.

He therefore rose, and went for a walk.

The fog parted obligingly before him; his feet quickly found a path, which became, in no more than a dozen steps, a very familiar path, indeed. He smiled as the last of the pale mists faded into a jumble of greens, browns, yellows, and reds, which coalesced into shrubberies and plantings of flowers that had entirely run wild, scattering everywhere, like so many unruly children, until the path surrendered, ceasing to be a path altogether, ending abruptly at a clearing enclosed by gloan roses; dominated by the trunk of an enormous tree.

A woman had her back and one booted foot against the vast trunk in a casual lean, arms crossed over her breast, the other foot braced against the ground. She was wearing a high necked sweater, and a pair of tough canvas pants—what had become the House at-home dress on chilly Surebleak. A long copper braid fell over one shoulder, bright against dark blue.

He grinned, his heart soaring, and went lightly across the clearing.

"*Cha'trez*," he murmured. "It is good to see you here."

"It's good to see you, here, too," she said, her smile soft as she raised a hand to his cheek. "Note that I'm madder'n a wet cat about that new trick of yours, but that's an argument for another day."

He frowned slightly, questing after recent memories—and found only a swirling of pink fogs.

"I believe that I am uninformed, in this time and place," he said. He caught her wrist and placed a kiss on the palm of her hand. "Forgive me."

"In this time and place? Sure."

"Excellent. I promise to accept my drubbing with courage, in that other time and place."

"Deal," she said, and closed the modest gap between them, her arms going 'round his waist. He returned the embrace, and willingly took part in the offered kiss, turning so that his back was against the Tree, feeling it warm him through jacket and shirt.

"What brings us here together?" he asked eventually.

Miri looked rueful.

"Me. I think. At least, I hoped I'd meet you here. You're in a 'doc at the Port Trauma Center right now."

She tipped her head.

"How much don't you remember?"

"A provocative question. I recall the arrival of the leader of the TerraTrade survey team, who wished to interview the Road Boss. She did so with objectiveness and efficiency, then rather spoiled the effect by pointing out that Korval's homeport, no matter where it might be, could not by definition be considered safe."

Miri blinked at him thoughtfully.

"Did you kill her?"

"Before she filed her report with TerraTrade? Credit me with some self-restraint."

She grinned.

"Sorry. Anything else?"

"Theo came next, aggrieved at the portmaster—" he paused, taking a sharp breath as the fogs parted and he remembered.

"The office was rushed. Nelirikk went down; Theo and I went out the bolt hole. They were waiting for us in the alley."

His blood chilled.

"Theo?" he breathed.

"She's alive. *Bechimo's* got a line on her; we know the name and location of the ship. But she's being held against her will, and the people holding her sent us her jacket—without her license. No note; no demands. Yet."

Yet, indeed. And so it was come.

He took a hard breath, and looked into Miri's face.

"The port is locked down?" he asked, knowing that a port lock-down was a meager deterrent at best.

"That's right. Got Scout patrols on duocycles. Got mercs on parade. Got the port cops on double-shifts."

"Do we know our enemy?"

Miri waggled her hand back and forth, meaning *yes* and, also, *no*.

"Looks like we got two actors—the DOI at the port, and Take Back Surebleak in the city. Or, if you like simplicity—one of the agents-in-place paid off a buncha bad actors to bust up things in the city, so it looked like Take Back Surebleak.

"Any case, there was windows busted, fires set, little bit of milling around—all *that* heavy lifting done by 'bleakers.

"Out from the city, some old company equipment all of a sudden woke up and went for a walk. *Bechimo* and Joyita put together a stop code pretty quick, there."

She took a breath, and met his eyes, clearly dreading her next revelation.

"yos'Galan's land was bombed."

"Of course it was," he said gently, and touched her cheek. "Have we casualties?"

"They hadn't quite got to work yet, at Shan's place. Melina said it woulda been a lot worse, if it'd happened during the growing season, or if the gadgets had made it into the village. As was, a storage shed was trashed, and some land got tore up before Bechimo turned 'em off.

"In the city, some broken bones. On port—you, Beautiful . . . and four corpses, none of 'em 'bleakers."

"So, the Department has decided to escalate," Val Con said; "and to hire out the work they cannot do themselves."

"You sound sure."

He extended a hand to catch her braid, delighting in the feel of warm, heavy silk against his palm.

"We expected this, after all," he murmured.

"We didn't expect *exactly* this," Miri protested.

"No, how could we? Flexibility is key." He smiled at her, raised the braid and kissed it.

"So. Our first priority is to make sure that the ship Theo is on cannot lift," he said.

"And, also, in the spirit of flexibility—I need to get out of that 'doc—now."

* * *

"You wasn't half too much trouble to pick up, was you, girly?"

The captain had grey in her cropped hair; two glittering white stones in her right ear; and grey eyes set wide on either side of a nose that had been broken at least once, and bent somewhat to the left.

She did not seem amused.

"I didn't ask you to pick me up," Theo pointed out reasonably.

"That's right. Got a client. Wanted you, him, or both. Nice bonus if we got both. Too bad about that. Cost me three crew and Rindle one. Fi was you, I'd stay outta Rindle's way; Patsy was something special to him."

"Am I likely to meet Rindle?"

"Hard to say. Port's on lockdown. Your 'count, I s'pose. Rindle was for taking you off just a soons we did the snatch. That's where it woulda been nice, we'd got both. Rindle coulda took one out and up, and seen 'em sold to *his* client. While me—I sat right here, just like I'm doin', an' collect money by the hour."

"If the port's on lock-down," Theo pointed out; "you can't lift, anyway."

"Oh, we could lift, if we wanted to lift. Ain't there, yet, is all. Just so long's that money comes in, the client can have it their way. They stop payin', we'll go, sure enough, and turn another a profit on you elsewhen."

"Why are you telling me this?" Theo asked.

"'cause I find people to be a deal less trouble to me when they unnerstan their proper place in the transaction. This is bidness, see, girly. My priority is to get paid. Got a client paying to keep you alive. Now, you might think that gives you a certain amount o'freedom to try my patience. What you need to know is you already tried my patience—Benny, Zama, and Feecher—they was old hands. Finding replacements and trainin' 'em up is gonna be spensive for me in a way the client's money don't cover. Client's contract is we gotta keep you alive, an', being the smart girly like you are, you'll see right off where that gives me a good deal o'latitude in your general condition."

"So, here's what you need to know. The client says alive, and the ribs're problematic. You might could do some damnfool thing and puncture a lung. So, we're gonna hafta see you in the ship's 'mergency unit for a minimum patch-up. We'll do that directly. First, though . . ."

She reached under the couch Theo was strapped to, and pulled out a pilot's jacket.

Her pilot's jacket, Theo saw, with outrage. She took a breath, felt a stab of pain; the room faded briefly, and came back, grey at the edges.

"See, now," the captain said. "You don't wanna be doing anything stupid; them ribs are cracked good. Can't stand shoddy work, m'self. Now, this jacket, here . . ."

"My jacket," Theo managed, her voice not steady.

"That's right," the captain said approvingly. "Your jacket, that the delm of Korval is gonna recognize every bit as quick as you did, just then. This jacket is gonna tell 'em not only we got you in hand, but you couldn't stop us takin' it offa you."

"So, you make the delm of Korval mad, then what?" Theo asked interestedly.

"The way the client tells the story, that jacket's gonna make the delm of Korval *scared*, girly. The client has it as an article of faith that the delm of Korval will do anything the client says, to keep you alive."

Theo was aware of a growing feeling of outrage, emanating from the area of bond-space. She took a breath, winced, and asked, "What happens if Korval decides not to play your client's game?"

Improbably, the captain smiled.

"That's a good question. The answer from the client's side is that we send along another little teaser that you wouldna give us, if you was able to resist. Say, a hand . . ." She paused, shrugged.

"It's been done, with a different client, unnerstan. Dunno the style of this present one, but that's the general gist o'the thing."

The outrage was approaching a boil.

"Calm down," she managed to say, in bond-space. "I need to think."

Bechimo's anger was gone, as if he'd closed a door between them.

Theo took a careful breath, mindful of the ribs. The captain nodded.

"So, we'll just be sending this along by courier, and while that's getting done, Jake'll get you set up in the 'doc."

The captain rose, and left.

Two minutes later, the door opened again, and here was the man with the scraped cheek and irritated eyes. Jake.

"What in space was that stuff you threw in my face?" he demanded, as he released the webbing.

"Tea," she told him.

"*Tea*!" He unhooked the wrist restraints from the couch, but not from around her wrists. Instead, he snapped the free ends together, to make one long leash.

"Right," Theo said. "*Bitter Truth* blend. Did you like it?"

He jerked her up by the wrist restraints; she didn't yell because she didn't have the breath to yell with, not then, and not when he pulled her off of the pallet, onto her feet.

She might've fallen, but he pushed hard against her, pinning her between himself and the couch.

"Don't be funny, girly, right? I don't like funny."

She got some air into her lungs, and managed to nod.

"Right," she said.

"That's a good girly," he said, with a grin. "You an' me're gonna get on just fine.

* * *

"We have a demand letter," Pat Rin said.

Natesa looked up from her screen.

"From . . .?"

"Take Back Surebleak, over the signature of *Boss Surebleak*."

Pat Rin met her eyes.

"A touch, you must admit."

"But I do not," she said. "Though I will admit that it is wonderful, how having an alias to hide behind emboldens the weak of character."

"You are harsh," he said, and looked back to the screen.

"Boss Surebleak demands that the Council of Bosses retire Conrad, and the Road Bosses. Children and adults of Clan Korval who were not involved in the invasion and hostile takeover of Surebleak will be allowed to leave the planet. All property of Conrad, and Clan Korval will be confiscated to partially offset the damage deliberately and maliciously done to a sovereign world."

He glanced up.

"All of this to be accomplished within the next two weeks, local."

Natesa leaned back in her chair, frowning.

"Someone," she said eventually, "has been tutoring *Boss Surebleak*."

"It does seem so, does it not?"

Pat Rin sighed.

"I will invite the Council of Bosses and the Road Boss to a remote conference in two hours. That will give everyone time to refresh themselves, and to become familiar with the terms."

* * *

Data flowed, building airy structures of possibility, which melted under the weight of discovered facts, or formed a core from those self-same facts and thus became, first, interesting, and then useful.

Joyita had quickly uncovered five of *Teramondi's* previous flight-names—impressive work, and so Jeeves praised it to him. However, Joyita, with his captain in peril, and *Bechimo* chafing to act, had turned his considerable talents into other channels thought to have more to do with the present emergency.

Jeeves had once spanned a planet, and had long ago developed subroutines—an entire bureaucracy of specialized protocols. He did not have the resources to span Surebleak, thus his planetary oversight duties consumed somewhat more computing power. But the little offices, the small efficiencies, that remained untapped were more than capable of tracking *Teramondi* down through all nine of the names it had flown under during a fifty-eight year career.

It had come into service as small trader *Light Star* out of Qwensi, under the command of one Vareta Jigs, captain-trader.

Trader Jigs developed and served a modestly profitable Short Loop for most of fifteen Standards; her fortunes changing when she was boarded by pirates, who presumably spaced the crew, of whom nothing else was ever discovered.

Light Star, however, rose again within the Standard as *Ysla* out of Waymart. She served the grey and black markets until an error in judgment brought unwanted attention upon her, whereupon she disappeared.

And appeared again not six Standards later, with a registration bought at Edmonton Beacon, for the good ship *Lalilokane*.

And so it went down the years.

The ship knew hard use by her numerous serial captains. Repair records included replacing damaged pod-mounts; tuning the drive engines; replacing the Struven unit; upgrading weapons systems; hull repair—and a replacement of the internal crisis system.

Teramondi, as she had been known for the last five Standards, had the hatch switches replaced at Selig Hulls. Selig Hulls yards—the company-owned yards, that was—produced competent work. Those yards which merely paid of fee in order to display the Selig Hulls logo, among others, in their advertising, in general, produced less competent work.

Teramondi, which at that time had been *Ankhor* out of Waymart, no longer even brushed the hems of the light worlds. Certainly, she was unlikely to come across a certified Seilg Hull repair facility.

Nor did she.

Thus, *Teramondi* had a vulnerability which could be exploited from a distance.

Jeeves considered the report Joyita had forwarded to him regarding Theo Waitley's condition. He would need to coordinate closely with *Bechimo* and Joyita, and also with the Pathfinders, who he understood were undertaking a rescue mission of their own devising.

Well enough, thought Jeeves. For this, the more confusion, the better. Though Bechimo insisted, and Jeeves agreed, that any action they undertook must wait until Theo Waitley had emerged from the autodoc.

* * *

Miri stirred.

"Won't do you much good, will it?," she asked her lifemate. "Way I heard it from the med tech, that arm's broke pretty good; plus some cuts and bruises; not to mention the gas you got into your lungs wasn't as nasty as it coulda been—but not by a lot."

"I believe that we have the means at hand to remedy many of these inconveniences," Val Con said.

The Tree, he meant. Which they'd talked about, with each other, and the Tree, too, while they were planning for this moment—or one not at all like it. There was just one problem.

"How'm I s'posed to get a pod into you, while you're locked in an autodoc in the Port Trauma Center?"

He blinked.

"Good question."

"That mean you don't have a good answer?"

"I—" Val Con started—and stopped, looking up into the branches above them.

Miri heard it, too, a long rustle, getting louder, as if of some object plummeting from a height through leaf and branch.

She stepped back; Val Con held out a hand. The pod hit his palm with a solid smack.

One pod; and it was his. She could tell by looking at it, and so could he. Even as she watched, the thing fell into quarters in his hand.

Miri looked up into the branches.

"*You* are an accessory to stupidity," she told the Tree. "And besides that, this ain't real; it's dream-time."

"Are we certain of that?" Val Con asked, dusting pod-shred off his fingers.

She glared at him.

"I sure went to sleep to get here."

"Yes, but that doesn't mean that we are *only* dreaming."

He took a step toward her—and hesitated, eyes narrowing.

"I'm being called back," he said, and closed the distance between them.

The kiss was urgent; rough; then he turned away, walking quickly across the clearing to the path—and was gone.

Chapter Nine

Surebleak Port

"Theo?" *Bechimo* sounded tentative inside her head.

"Right here," she said.

"You were *gone*," he said.

"They put me in a 'doc," she said, remembering that much. She opened her eyes, and considered the pale glow a few inches above her face. "Still there, looks like."

"What is your condition?"

"Good question."

She took a deep breath. Some residual ache, but no stabbing pain. The knee was sore, but nothing that would prevent her from walking, running, or even kicking, if it came to that. Her hands were stiff; experimentally, she flexed her fingers, and something heavy and slick ran across her palm.

Anger sparked.

"What is it?" *Bechimo* asked, sharply.

"Idiot put me into the 'doc with the restraints on. I guess he's not taking any chances." She took another breath; sighed it out.

"Other than that, I'm in good enough shape. I'm going to open the lid."

"Wait!" *Bechimo* said. "Theo, you must hold yourself ready. We are going to get you off of that ship. You must be ready to run, when I say the word."

"In that case," she said; "I'd better get this lid up."

The strap linking her wrists wasn't tight, but it didn't give her much play, either. She had to move both hands more or less together, which was awkward. With a little wriggling, she was able to reach the right side of the compartment, where the release lever should have been.

But wasn't.

Theo muttered, and squirmed 'round onto her back again.

Some models, she remembered, had a latch on the inside of the lid. She raised her bound hands, groping, and failed to locate a latch. A shove directly against the lid failed to pop it.

She was locked in.

"Theo, your heartbeat just spiked."

"The lid's locked," she said. "I guess they don't want me wandering around on my own. It makes sense, really. I'm in no danger."

Good thing I don't have claustrophobia, she thought. Her childhood best friend, Lesset, had a horror of being confined in the dark; she'd been assigned to take therapy for it. Back then, Theo had a long list of physical disabilities on file with the Safety Office, but she'd never been afraid of small spaces, or the dark.

"We will wait to act until you are at liberty," *Bechimo* said. There was a pause, and he said, tentatively, "Would you like me to stay with you?"

She wasn't afraid of the dark, Theo thought. On the other hand, it would be good to know that she wasn't alone.

"Yes," she said. "I'd like that a lot."

"All right," said *Bechimo*; he hesitated, and then asked, "Would you like to listen to music?"

Theo took a breath. The inside of the 'doc *hadn't* gotten any smaller, she told herself. It was just that the light had faded, a little.

"Tell me a story," she said.

"A story?" *Bechimo* sounded startled. "I don't know any stories."

"Sure you do. Where did you go, after you'd saved yourself, and before you met Win Ton? You must've seen some interesting things." She paused, and decided to risk teasing him a little.

"You didn't stay in your safe place *all* the time, did you?"

"Not... *all* of the time," *Bechimo* said after a moment.

There was another pause, though she could still feel his presence in bound-space.

"Well," *Bechimo* said then, and his voice had something of Clarence's lilt to it. "Now that you mention it, I do remember the time I was over near the edge of the Dust, and I happened upon another ship, like me..."

* * *

A chime was going off in his ear, progressively louder. Val Con opened his eyes to behold a very worried, very Terran, face above him.

"You're healed?" said the face, sounding equal parts disbelieving and horrified.

"The machine seems to think so," Val Con answered; "but it is prudent to be certain of these things. A moment."

He lay still for a moment, taking stock; there was, he noticed, a lingering taste of Tree-fruit along his tongue. Other than that, he felt no pain, nor weakness in his limbs; he breathed easily, with no burning in his lungs.

Carefully, he raised his arms. The face hastily retreated, and he used the momentum of the stretch to pull himself into a sitting position.

He felt perfectly well.

"Apparently," he said to the med tech; "I am healed."

"But it's hours too soon;" the tech protested. He turned away, as Val Con rolled out of the 'doc, landing effortlessly on his feet.

The tech turned back, clutching a diagnostic pad.

"The inventory of injuries, and the projected time to heal," he said, shoving the pad under Val Con's nose.

Politely, he glanced at the screen.

"Yes, I see—a nine hour repair. How long has it been?"

"Five," said the med tech, snatching the pad back and staring at the readout. "Five hours, and you're completely—that's *not possible*."

"And, yet, it seems to have happened. Perhaps the machine needs recalibration."

"I guess it does! Putting that order in right now!" His attention on the screen, he started out of the cubicle; paused and looked over his shoulder.

"Your wife sent down some clothes that don't have blood and muck on 'em," he said. "They're in the press." He paused, eyes narrowed. "Might be best if you just had something to eat in the caf, here, and stay where we can see you for the next hour. Just in case something's *really* screwy with that 'doc."

"Thank you," Val Con said. "I will undertake to do nothing beyond my abilities." He thought he heard something very like Miri's disbelieving snort at the back of his mind—gone before he could decide if it had come through the lifemate link, or was merely his supposition of her likely reaction.

The tech, meanwhile, his attention already back on the data-pad, left the cubicle.

Val Con surveyed the area, concluded that "the press" was the small mobile closet, and opened the door.

Very shortly, he was dressed in a dark, high-necked sweater; tough canvas pants; and his own boots, which would need to be cleaned, but would do for the moment. His jacket . . . there was a brush on the shelf at the top of "the press," and he spent a few minutes applying it vigorously. Space leather was tough, and pilots tended to take pride in the scars and stains their jackets accumulated. Sticky alley scum was another thing altogether, and he was pleased that most of it yielded to the ministrations of the brush.

He checked the pockets, finding everything in its place, nothing missing; and was about to swing the jacket on when it—buzzed.

Frowning, he slipped his hand into a semi-public pocket on the inside right, and pulled out a Scout-issue close-range comm unit.

He thumbed it on.

"yos'Phelium."

"Master Val Con, excellent," Jeeves said, sounding positively buoyant. "We are preparing to remove Captain Waitley from her predicament aboard *Teramondi*. Are you in a position to assist?"

"As a matter of fact, I am. What do you have planned?"

* * *

"*Boss Surebleak*," Boss Schroeder snorted. "We're s'posed to take this serious, are we?"

"Oh, I think we gotta take it serious," Penn Kalhoon said. "Did a bit o'damage today on my streets, and the fact that we didn't get anything more fatal than a broken arm from it wasn't necessarily in the Boss's plan."

"That's a surety," said Melina Sherton; "assuming it's Boss Surebleak who got them machines walking over Tapout way.

They'd've crushed Gapton Village if we hadn't got some friendly intervention from Captain Waitley's comm officer."

"Doin' what?" asked Boss Wentworth.

"Got into the command-line and issued a stop order," said Melina.

"Somebody's smarter'n new snow," said Fortunato. "How'd the machines get started up first off?"

Melina shrugged.

"Remote signal, just like what stopped 'em. There's a set o'manual override keys, but I know where they are, an' ain't nobody touched 'em since the day I come Boss."

"Remote signal," said Boss Vine. "We got so many remote signals flyin' around late days, there's no sayin' but that one of *them* triggered the machines, accidental."

"Maybe," said Melina. "I'll hold it as a consideration. But my first inclination is to count the machines in with the rest of today's antics. Boss Surebleak hit wide, but, what's specially inneresting to me is that they hit the territories of the Old Bosses who threw in with Conrad."

There was silence.

Melina looked around at the other Bosses, each in their screen.

"Well?" she said; "ain't that so? Penn Kalhoon, me, Ira, Wentworth. An' that's before we get to lookin' at the port—who got hit there?" She raised her hand, fingers extended, and folded down one with each word—"Emerald. Mack's. Road Boss. Portmaster. Conrad and his brother; and their two biggest supporters, portside. Does that look like *random* to any of you?"

Boss Whitmore broke this silence.

"Gotta assume it's all related, 'til we have more info. Trouble's gonna be gettin' more info before Boss Surebleak turns testy and starts up another round of zample-makin.'"

"We don't know there hasn't already been another round," said Schroeder, glumly.

"I think that we would be informed, if there had been another series of attacks," said Conrad gently. "I also think that we may expect no more attacks today. Boss Surebleak has issued demands, and a deadline by which those demands must be met. Therefore, while we may perhaps except a slowly escalating scale of small mischiefs, as the deadline comes closer, I believe that the streets are safe enough for at least the next few days."

"So, what's that get us?" asked Engle.

"We have time to write a letter of our own . . ." Conrad frowned. "No, perhaps, we will take a notice in the newspapers, as Boss Surebleak did not include her direction in the letter."

"A notice in the newspapers saying what?" Penn Kalhoon asked, fair brows drawn together.

"Why, stating that the Counsel of Bosses is in receipt of Boss Surebleak's letter, and wish to discuss the list of demands with the Boss personally at the special working lunch meeting called for mid-week."

Penn blinked.

"They'll come in shootin,'" said Vine. "If they come at all."

"Perhaps. Or perhaps not. We can but make the effort."

More silence, as the assembled Bosses each turned the idea over and examined it.

"It's what we gotta do," said Ira abruptly. "That's what people do, they have differences; they try to work 'em out. Give a little, get a little; nobody's happy, but everybody's still standing. If we don't want Surebleak took back to the way it was, then we gotta do different from the Old Bosses."

There was a general murmur of agreement. Conrad inclined his head.

"I will draft a notice for the papers, and send it to each of you no later than tomorrow morning. Comments and suggestions may come back to me before sundown. I will place the approved notice in the papers tomorrow night, and it will run beginning in the daylight editions on the day after tomorrow."

He glanced 'round at each face in its screen.

"Does that meet with the approval of the Council?"

Ayes were given, and Conrad stood.

"In that case, I bid you all good-day. Let us be watchful, and stay in touch. If it comes about that there is more mischief, please contact Penn Kalhoon with a detailed report. He will keep a list and share it with council members."

That, too, gained approval, and one by one the screens went dark as the Bosses signed out of the conference.

Pat Rin sat down again with a long sigh, and met Natesa's eyes.

"Do you intend to retire Boss Surebleak?" she asked.

He gave her a wry smile.

"No. But before you paint me with virtue, it is only because a retirement will not solve the problem. Retire one Boss Surebleak, and a second will arise, stronger than the first. We must find another way. And, also—"

He gave her a light, seated, bow.

"We need to discover who is giving Boss Surebleak her lessons."

* * *

The story had been fascinating as much for the things *Bechimo* didn't say as those that he did. And apparently the Dust was even stranger that she'd supposed it must be.

"Is that even true?" Theo asked, half-drowsily.

"Of course, it's true!" *Bechimo* said, doing a really good job of sounding outraged at this impugning of his honor. "I cannot lie."

She laughed.

"I might've believed you if you hadn't added that."

"Truly?"

"Truly. Ask yourself if Clarence would've ever said that."

"He would—he has! He places his hand over his heart, and—"

Theo laughed again, remembering.

"He does, doesn't he? And manages to look offended and coy at the same time, too!"

"Perhaps there is a tone of voice that is both offended and coy," Bechimo said. "I will research the problem."

"You do that," she said cordially. "I want to hear it when you—"

The 'doc was flooded with brilliant light; Theo reflexively threw up one hand to shield her eyes, the binders tangled briefly, and she hit herself in the nose.

Blinded by the light, she heard a grating noise, felt the movement of air against her face; started to sit up—

And was slammed back on to the pallet.

The breath left her lungs in a shout, and a hand came down hard over her mouth.

"Miss me, Blondie?" said the unwelcome voice of Jake, with the scraped cheek and the red eyes.

Theo bit his thumb.

He swore, slapped her face with the wounded hand and twisted the binding cord in his other hand, jerking her arms over her head.

Theo grit her teeth; her eyes were still dazzled, but she could make out a dark shape leaning close above her, feel his breath, coming fast, against her face.

"So, you liked bein' left alone in the dark, didja? We'll see if we can't put you back, after we have some fun."

He tightened the cord; she gasped, and tried to twist.

"That's right; I like a feisty girl," Jake said, and jerked her sweater up, his fingers closing over her breast like a vise.

Distantly, she was aware of *Bechimo's* fury; a paltry flame against her own bonfire of outrage.

Jake was leaning over her, his weight on the pallet, controlling her by keeping the cord taut. She had to move before he brought his weight into play.

"How 'bout a kiss for lettin' you outta the dark?"

His mouth came down on hers; tongue invading—and his grip on the cord slackened, just enough.

Theo twisted, got her legs up and kicked.

It wasn't a solid hit, but it knocked him back—and he dropped the cord.

"Why, you little bitch."

She heard the snap of a flip-knife opening, and kicked again, knocking him back, using the momentum to snap upright, both fists before her, and punching as hard as she could.

There was a snap, like a piece of plastic breaking. Theo kicked a third time and rolled out of the 'doc, landing awkwardly, one foot skidding on—

Her eyes were mostly clear now, and she could see that she'd skidded on the flip-knife.

Jake . . .

Jake was down, his neck at a bad angle.

The door to the alcove snapped open.

Theo swooped, snatched up the knife, and came up into a crouch, hands close.

Framed in the doorway, the captain gave her a nod.

"You're no end spensive, ain't you, girly?"

"He was—" Theo begin—and stopped when the captain moved her hand in a sharp *abort*!

"I seen it. Din't say I blamed you, but I'm getting' low on crew." She paused, squinting.

"Normal times, you'd earnt that knife, but you ain't crew; and times ain't normal. I can take it away from you—an' I *can* take it away from you—or you can slide it over here, polite-like."

"Theo," *Bechimo* said in bond-space. "Do not risk yourself."

But Theo had already bent over to send the knife skittering over the decking.

"Smart girl."

The captain picked up the knife and tucked it into her belt. Straightening, she nodded at what was left of Jake.

"Place wants tidying. You stay right there, an' I'll send Lyn down to supervise that."

* * *

"Now," said Chernak, and swung out into the row of ships, walking briskly, satchel in hand. Stost, at her side, was similarly attired in coveralls with MACK'S stitched onto the right breast. He wore a tool belt.

The coveralls were Andy Mack's contribution to *pay-back*, as he had it, and, with sleeves rolled and legs tucked into boots, could be made to look as if they fit.

So, two of Mack's repair techs on their way to a job, tool-belts jingling.

"Do you wish them to hear us coming, my Stost?" Chernak asked.

"In the usual way of things, Elder, would repair techs not walk hard, tools ringing?"

She considered that, and altered her own gait until her bootheels hit the 'crete smartly.

"You are correct," she said.

This was fully for the benefit of those who they might meet in the short walk down to the pad where *Teramondi* sat, outwardly innocent.

Teramondi's sensors, as well as the sensors of all the other ships in this row, and the port's own sensors—failed to record their passage. This was Joyita's doing, with assistance from Clarence. But even they could not override the sensors for long. Soon or late, someone would note that the feed was blank, and try to reboot.

Best they were done and well-away before that occurred.

They arrived at the correct pad, swung under the gantry, and were immediately invisible.

* * *

Val Con finished his tea, carried the cup to the washer, and left the caf by the side door. It was a crisp afternoon, naturally enough, and the Trauma Center had been very warm, by Surebleak standards. He finished with the underarm pocket, sealed the jacket, turned the collar up and pulled on the gloves he had stowed in the cargo pockets. That done, he tucked his hands in those same pockets, and leaned against the wall, waiting.

He let his attention touch the song that was Miri—the manifestation of the lifemate link—and allowed it to soothe him.

Miri was not happy with the plan, which, truthfully, could scarcely be dignified by the word. At the moment, they stood very much at a disadvantage, forced to react to their opponent's moves, rather than setting the tempo themselves. That, of course, would need to change, but first, the board must be cleared of unnecessary pieces. Theo, for instance, was not meant to have been in the game at all.

That she had been taken, and held at the whim of the Department—was, he admitted to himself—horrifying. And while he was reasonably certain that there was no agent of the DOI on *Teramondi* at the moment, he was far less certain that this would continue to be the case.

Thus, an immediate extraction was called for.

The odds of that succeeding were very good, indeed, he noted. The follow—well, there. They were forced to dance to a tune of another's choosing, and for the follow, he was reduced to—hope.

A sound from the real world intruded upon his thoughts—a low, growling purr, moving up the street toward his place against the wall.

He opened his eyes and straightened as the duocycle gently rounded the corner, and nosed in to park against the wall.

A figure in space leather swung out of the saddle, landing somewhat unsteadily, and stood for a moment, hand on the bar, until she had her balance back.

Val Con moved forward, and the Scout looked up, her face grim and weary.

"Long shift?" Val Con asked her, in Comrade mode.

She grimaced.

"I've done longer, though not while dodging stones and sticks and garbage," she said. "The portmaster has us on short circuits, to diminish the opportunity for malice to spring up between sweeps. Not a bad plan, on the face of it. However, knowing the timing and the route does provide occasion for merriment among the ne'er-do-wells."

"Riots?"

"I judge not. Just the local bad element having a bit of fun at our expense."

"Ah."

He used his chin to point at the cycle.

"It happens I have business down-port. May I borrow that?"

She considered him frankly.

"You *are* the reason I was ordered to break route at the Trauma Center for tea and a rest period, aren't you?"

He smiled.

"Yes."

She nodded, and turned toward the cycle.

"An innovation, perhaps, since the last time you rode."

She pointed at a lever set at the joining of the handlebars.

"Turn that as far as it will go to the left and the machine will produce a nerve-shattering roar, which even the local bad element are inclined to take seriously. Nudge it up just a mark, and the cycle produces that delightful low growl that alerted you to my presence."

"Yes, thank you; that is a new feature."

"Also," the Scout said; "the tires are Surebleak weight, for more traction in snow and ice."

She looked back to him, and moved her shoulders.

"Other than that, it's the same design you and I stealthily borrowed from the academy's inventory in order to go joy-riding 'round Solcintra Port."

"Excellent," he said; "I have fond memories."

"As I do."

She gave him a brief nod.

"If you wish to enjoy the ride, avoid the old refinery section. There are quite a number of ne'er-do-wells congregated there, and their target is the cycle. Rider down is plainly their goal."

"I will be careful," he said, softly.

She laughed.

"I believe you."

He watched her open the door and enter the caf before he swung up into the saddle and kicked the starter.

* * *

Theo was on her knees on the cold decking, cleaning out Jake's pockets, while Lyn leaned against the wall, stun-gun out, watching.

Jake hadn't been a pilot, but his jacket had just as many pockets, and then there were more in his pants. Mostly, he had money—not much of any one kind, but at least a dozen different currencies, including Surebleak cash.

He also had a complete set of finger-knives, a tin of *vya*, another tin of, according to the label across the top, *All Fine*, six flats of brightly colored pills, a smoke bomb, and a thumb-gun.

Among other things.

Theo finally sat back on her heels, and used both hands to push her hair out of her face.

"I think that's everything," she said.

Lyn shook her head.

"Had a couple necklaces he always wore; an' the belt's got some kinda trick to it," said Lyn, not moving.

Theo sighed, reached for Jake's shirt and unsealed it.

Three chains in three different metals around his neck; a leather bracelet with a name burned into it—Sal Zar ter'Eazon—the belt, all required some persuasion, but at last Theo sat back on her heels.

"Anything else?" she asked.

Lyn peered in to the box.

"Gods, he was still wearin' that thing?" she muttered, and looked up.

"That piece o'space leather, there, tells you everything you need to know about Jake. Killed a pilot—first kill, the way he tol' the story. An' he made him a bracelet outta the jacket, with the name on."

Shaking her head, she eased back against the wall.

"People pay good money for spaceleather, 'specially the jackets. Don't matter it's some scratches or stains—space! some'd pay *more* for the damage. Coulda sold it for upwards of a cantra, all he hadda do was be patient and pick his port." She shook her head in disgust.

"Not Jake, though. No, ma'am. He'd rather have that *victory bracelet* to prop up his legend."

She snorted.

"*Legend*. Somebody shoulda wasted his legend long years ago."

Theo didn't say anything, but Lyn looked at her hard.

"Don't be getting any ideas like I'm owing you. We don't play by them rules."

"'course not," Theo said mildly. "Is that everything, now?"

"Don't see nothing not there that oughta be," Lyn said; "an' you hit every pocket I could see."

She straightened up and jerked the stun-gun at Theo.

"On your feet and grab aholt, there, girly. Jake's going down to the 'cycler, where he'll finally be doin' some good."

#

Theo's ribs were aching by the time she got Jake to the recycling room, and she straightened slowly, taking a couple of deep breaths.

"You need to rest," *Bechimo* told her.

"What's the hold-up?" Lyn snapped.

"Taking a breather," she said, keeping her voice mild.

"You can get your breather after you get Jake situated."

Theo held up her hands, showing the cord that bound them together.

"Can I get some help? Maybe you could take off the bindings?"

Lyn shifted, showing the stun-gun.

"Or maybe you could stop stalling and get the job done? It'll be tougher after you come up from bein' stunned, but if you're workin' the challenge level, I'll help you, sure."

Theo counted to twelve, which didn't do anything at all for *her* temper, and visibly increased Lyn's irritation.

"I can't operate the mechanism with my hands bound like this," Theo said. "That's just a fact, and it won't change, no matter how many times you stun me."

She waited, already feeling the bolt crackle along her nerve endings.

Lyn huffed, reached into her pouch and jerked her head.

"Come over here and hold out your arms."

Theo stepped forward.

"That's close enough!"

"Right." She extended her hands.

Lyn raised a little device that was barely any bigger than her thumb, and pressed it.

There was a slight sigh, and the binders fell from Theo's wrists.

"Thanks," she said.

"You're on borrowed time, girly, and the minute Jake's took care of, it's going back on, right?"

"Right," muttered Theo, turning toward the recycling unit.

THUMP

"What the—" yelled Lyn, spinning around toward the door, stun-gun ready, like she'd fire at the next noise.

"Theo," *Bechimo* said inside her head. "You must go *now* to the nearest exit. It will be open."

"Which will be open?" she demanded, stepping around Jake's body.

"All of them."

"Right," she said aloud.

Lyn turned.

"Get away from me, girly," she snarled, raising the stun-gun.

Theo socked her in the jaw.

* * *

THUMP.

On her way to the bridge, Captain Lisle staggered, straightened, and broke into a run.

"All hands, all hands!" Ruzo's voice came over the intercom. "We have a breach. Repeat, the hull has been breached!"

She hit the wall-switch.

"Lisle. Details."

"Captain. Hull breached at four pressure points, internal and external."

"Recording?"

"Camera's dead," Ruzo said.

Lisle swore.

A gentle *bong* sounded in over the speaker, reverberating slightly. The door on the tool station next to the intercom silently swung open.

"Breach!" Ruzo snapped again. "All hatches open!"

"What!" Lisle stared down a hall lined with open doors—utility stations, the door to the galley; the door to her own stateroom . . .

"Interior hatches?" she asked Ruzo.

"Negative—*all*," came the reply; then—

"Visitor at the main hatch," she said, just as the annunciator sounded.

Captain Lisle turned and ran toward the main hatchway.

* * *

Chernak pressed the annunciator button once more and settled comfortably at a slight angle to the hatch. She had not taken cover, but she was not precisely where she would be expected to be, and that was all the advantage she needed, should the person who eventually arrived from inside the ship fire before thinking.

There came from within the sound of hasty feet, and a well-grown woman of the sort called Terran rounded the corner and approached the hatch.

She slowed, gun in hand, and—stopped, just inside the open hatchway.

To her credit, she did not fire.

In fact, she froze, looking at Chernak's face, her own gone pale.

"Soldier," she croaked.

"My reputation proceeds; it is well," said Chernak affably. "Surrender your weapon."

She was obeyed without hesitation, which was interesting, Chernak thought. According to the records Joyita had found, this woman did not surrender easily.

Chernak took the offered weapon by its butt, and slid it away into a pocket. There was a slight tremor under her boots, and Stost arrived on the gantry at her side.

"Star hammer!" he cried, brandishing that tool in both hands.

Chernak smiled.

"Do you claim it as a prize? Kara will be pleased."

"Put that down!" snapped Captain Lisle. "I gave my gun to this soldier; I'm unarmed!"

There was a moment of silence before Stost hefted the hammer, grinning like the fool he was not.

"As I am!" he said jovially. "Shall we try, unarmed, each against the other?"

Chapter Ten

Surebleak Port

Val Con had quite liked duocycles when he had been a hopeful Scoutling at academy. Indeed, he had taken the prize in several duocycling competitions—both illicit and academy-sponsored.

Even as a Scout about his duty, he had retained a fondness for the little machines, which could move so quickly, and so quietly, over many kinds of terrain.

Today, however . . .

The frigid wind slapped his face until it burned; his nose went numb, and his eyes teared, despite the goggles, which led to the lenses steaming up and providing a serious impediment to safe duocycling. He yanked them down to dangle 'round his neck, and crouched low over the handlebars.

Perhaps he was growing old.

Ahead, a cluster of people.

Val Con made use of the innovation, producing a roar that echoed off the buildings on either side, and had people scrambling for positions of lesser peril.

"Hey!" one woman yelled as he raced by. "Watch where you're goin'!"

He grinned into the wind.

Well, perhaps not quite so old as that.

"Turn left at the next intersection," Jeeves said into his ear.

He took the corner fast, nearly putting the cycle on its side, straightened, and roared again, hearing answering roars from ahead, behind, and to the side.

Turning his head slightly, he saw two duocycles on his right hand; two more on his left—and even more racing in from the side streets as he stormed past.

"Jeeves, am I part of a parade?"

"A diversionary tactic, sir. You will concentrate on picking up Captain Waitley. These others will provide cover, and create confusion."

"More confusion," he said; "delightful."

"Yes, sir."

He loosed another roar. Two dozen and more answered him, and they sped on, the port itself vibrating with their challenge.

* * *

Captain Lisle looked at the star hammer; she looked, very carefully, Chernak thought, at Stost, her gaze flicking between his eyes and his grin several times.

Finally, as if she had found him an irrefutable argument, she turned back to Chernak.

"What do you want?"

"I believe you should lay out your weapons," Chernak said. "Tell me where they are before you reach to them, so that my comrade does not misunderstand."

That was unjustly said; Stost had a very fine understanding of nuance and body language—better than her own. However, it was to their advantage to encourage Captain Lisle's uneasiness.

"Knife," the captain said. "Right boot."

She was methodical. Knives came out first—three of them—then a small arm, and a second—

"That," Stost said, hefting the star hammer, "is our captain's own sidearm!"

Chernak had also recognized it, and held up her hand. There was sweat on Captain Lisle's face.

"You will not move," Chernak told her. "You will keep your arms at your sides, and your hands where I can see them."

"Right," Captain Lisle said.

"Stost, retrieve our captain's weapon," she directed.

He did this, adroitly, and stepped back, tucking the gun away, and hefting the hammer.

"The rest," Chernak said to Captain Lisle.

She produced two more guns, then stood back, arms crossed over her breast.

"What do you want?" she demanded, which was, Chernak thought, more like the woman Joyita had found in his searches.

"First," Chernak said, "we wanted to ensure that this ship would not lift."

"Well, you managed that just fine, from what my pilot tells me. Then what?"

Chernak cocked her head, listening. Yes, there was a growling in the streets, growing rapidly closer.

"Then," she told Captain Lisle, "we wanted to hold you for the port guards."

"You don't want your captain back?"

"No, we do want our captain back," said Chernak.

The growling was closer now; she saw Captain Lisle notice the racket, and frown.

"Call off the proctors and I'll hand over your captain," she said.

This was the offer that the entire crew had supposed she would make, that they had determined that they could not take, if they wished to have their captain back—*alive.*

"Will you call her up to us?" asked Chernak, and felt Stost shift at her back.

"Sure; I'll send one of my crew down to bring her up. How's that? I'd appreciate a little something to cover my losses, since my client ain't gonna pay if he don't get what he wanted. But, I'm sure we can make a—"

Chernak saw the woman's arms, crossed so casually over her chest, tighten, very slightly. She swept out a leg, the captain staggered—and Chernak had her on her knees, arms pinned at her side.

"Gas canisters!" she snapped. "Stost, your hammer."

"No!" yelled Captain Lisle, jerking ineffectually against Chernak's prisoning arms.

"Fool," said Stost, and brought his knuckle sharply against her temple.

They laid Captain Lisle's unconscious body on the gantry. Chernak bent to remove the canisters—

And the duocycles arrived.

* * *

Crew was on the move, Theo discovered; and they were looking for her.

She'd found a pole, and slid down to the maintenance level, dodging into a utility alley that felt thin even to her. It was a maze of open doors and exposed panels, which would work to hide her, if-and-when crew decided to pursue her, but—

"What happened?" she asked *Bechimo*.

"The Pathfinders have assured that this ship will not lift," he told her. "You are approaching a T-corridor. When it is safe to do so, go left."

Theo paused at end of her skinny alley, straining her ears.

Voices. She heard voices, approaching. Ducking back into the alley, she wedged herself into a tall closet, behind a portable air compressor.

She heard the steps slow, and stop at the top of the alley. Heard the voices consult with one another. One came a few steps into the alley, stopped, then retreated.

"Don't see no boots on deck," he said. "I'm bettin' she's headed straight for the emergency slide. No sense getting' tangled up in that mess in there."

The footsteps faded.

Theo slipped out of the closet, ran lightly to the T and took the left, making for, so *Bechimo* had assured her, the utility hatch.

"What's happening up top?" she asked *Bechimo*.

"Captain Lisle and the Pathfinders are seeking common ground," he told her. "Turn right at the approaching corner. You will be next to the ship's skin. Continue to follow the curve of the hallway. The hatch is not far from your current position."

Theo took a deep breath, spotting a camera in a corner of the ceiling. *Bechimo* had told her that the cameras were "momentarily offline," but seeing it there still gave her a nasty thrill.

While she was on this ship, she was still a hostage, and whatever might be happening between the captain and the pathfinders, up at the main hatch, all agreements would be off, if she was captured again.

Theo ducked around the last corner—

And came face-to-face with Lyn.

"Got you!" the crew woman snarled, raising a merc-issue pellet pistol.

Theo threw herself to the right and down, twisted and brought the stun gun up.

Lyn might've been able to get one shot off—Theo wasn't sure. But she didn't get two.

Theo came to her feet, feeling a stab of pain along her ribs.

"Quickly," *Bechimo* urged, and she gathered herself into a trot after she collected the pellet gun.

Follow the passage, curving, curving—and there, ahead, a small hatch hanging loosely open like all the others. A damp, chilly breeze rubbed past her cheek, smelling like grit and fuel and smoke and snow.

Theo stretched her legs, aware of a roaring sound even as she came to the opening, and flung a hand out to the nearest grab bar. Crouching, she measured the jump from hatch to 'crete.

She could do it, she judged, though she found herself wishing for her jacket. If she landed badly, all there was between her and the 'crete was a sweater. Still, she should be able to walk away, once she got . . .

"Theo?"

"Thinking," she said. "I think I can make the jump, but—"

"Hold position," *Bechimo* said. "Your brother is coming for you."

And, as if on cue, there came a deafening roar as a mob of duocycles swept into the lane below.

"He is here," *Bechimo* said, sounding very pleased with himself.

"Him and two dozen of his friends," she answered, "how am I supposed to—"

She stopped, because the cycles were splitting up, swinging wide, half to the left of the ship and half to the right.

One, however, came straight on, *slowing*, maybe, but not by any means traveling slow.

"Jump!" cried *Bechimo*. "Theo, jump *now*!"

* * *

Val Con swerved close, slowing, saw the jacketless figure in the hatch flex her knees—and leap.

The stabilizers groaned when she hit the saddle behind him, then her arms were around his waist and he kicked the accelerator.

"Head down!" he shouted, and felt her curl close against his back, letting him take the worst of the wind and grit.

They had lost all but two of their escort—a cycle flanking them on either side. Well, enough, he thought, if they could keep up.

* * *

The last time Theo had been on a duocycle had been at school, and only then because she needed the training to get her certs for Port-Side Machinery. Some of her classmates had seen the challenge in the little machines, and had engaged in races, acrobatics, and crazy mid-night tours of the dark grounds.

Theo had not been one of those.

But apparently Val Con had.

She'd barely dropped into the saddle before he hit the accelerator, flying low, and she grabbed his waist to steady herself. Now, she settled herself more firmly into the saddle, and took hold of the passenger handgrips.

Val Con shifted slightly before her, turning his head slightly.

"Theo!" The wind thinned his voice; she leaned closer, to hear.

"Right underarm pocket—small weapon!"

Weapon—that was, she thought, exactly like him. Of course, he'd want to make sure she was armed.

Carefully, she eased her hand up, found the pocket, and fingered out a small, surprisingly heavy, pouch. She got it firmly in hand, and slid it into her leg pocket. The duocycle was solid as a rock, which she thought was more Val Con's doing than hers. She sealed the pocket and put her arm back around his waist.

"Got it!" she yelled, though she was pretty sure he couldn't hear her. "Thanks!"

They were running quiet now—no roaring, only the low hum of the motor. She caught a movement out of the corner of her eye, and turned her head. Another cycle was pacing them on the left—a second on the right, both drivers leather-clad, faces obscured by goggles. Backup, she supposed. Good idea.

Val Con leaned, and she did; the cycle almost perpendicular to the 'crete, shooting into a side-way with no lessening of speed. They snapped upright, Val Con hunched over the handlebars, and Theo taking care to keep her arms inside the cycle's shadow. The walls were *that* close.

Up ahead, she could see the end of the alley over Val Con's shoulder. There seemed to be a lot of people about.

"*Bechimo*," she said in bond-space. "What's going on?"

"Flash-crowd," he said tensely. "This a rarely used section, which is why Jeeves routed you through it."

"So, somebody's still really interested in what we're doing," Theo said.

"That is one theory," *Bechimo* answered. "There is no way around; it must be through. Jeeves allows me to know that your brother is very skilled with the duocycle."

"Good," she said, and there wasn't any time to say more, because they burst into the street, Val Con swinging the cycle hard to the left, and it was roaring again, but the crowd was roaring almost as loud, and a couple of people jumped in front of them, which was a dare, Theo knew—

And Val Con kicked the accelerator.

"Sleet, man, are you crazy?" screamed one of them, as they leapt aside, and hit the 'crete, rolling.

The duocycle roared again, echoes coming from behind, which was their escort, Theo thought. Val Con didn't let up, his course straight and unhesitant. More people jumped out of their way, they hit a clear space—

And something came in low, rolling across the 'crete, too near to jump over. It hit the front wheel; the cycle skittered, slid; Val Con brought it back up by sheer willpower, so it seemed to Theo, and here came another one, at the back wheel.

Theo took a breath, deliberately relaxing into the cycle's dance, trying to forget that she didn't have a jacket, only a sweater and canvas pants between her and the 'crete.

I need meteor shields, she thought, even as something caught the edge of her eye—another damn' roller, coming in fast, about an inch above the 'crete—

The cycle bucked, and for a moment, it felt like the machine was trying to swim.

"Jump!" Val Con snapped, and she did, hitting the ground with arms over her head, rolling, and it didn't hurt as much as she'd expected, which was maybe adrenaline—

There came a terrible grinding noise; the scream of abused stabilizers—and a roar from the crowd that was louder than anything Theo had ever heard in her life.

She opened her eyes, got up on one knee, braced on her hands. The crowd was surging forward, apparently having forgotten that there had been two riders. There was a downed cycle a sort distance away, also ignored. The mob was focused elsewhere.

Nobody was paying any attention to her.

She got both feet under her, and bolted to the duocycle, keeping low until she had it by the handlebars; shoving it up onto its wheels, and straddling it—only then realizing that the safety program had shut it off when it went down, and she didn't have the code.

"Wait," *Bechimo* said. And, "here."

The inside of her head *tickled*; and she glanced down in time to see her fingers finish inputting something into the keypad. The duocycle purred to life; Theo kicked the accelerator, spinning in a hard turn, until she was facing the surging crowd.

"Theo!" *Bechimo* cried.

"Val Con's down!" she shouted back at him. "This crowd will kill him!"

A duocycle came speeding in from the right of the crowd, roar at full volume; another right behind.

Theo pulled up, one boot braced against the 'crete.

Somebody in the crowd screamed; people scrambled; shoved, and shouted as the lead cycle pierced it like an arrow, scattering them, shouting and cursing. Theo saw somebody on the ground, arms around head, motionless. Her mouth dried—and then he was moving, spinning up into a crouch as the second cycle slowed, the operator holding down an arm.

Val Con grabbed the offered support, and swung onto the pillion, as the cycle accelerated, flying to catch up with the leader.

"He's safe, Theo;" *Bechimo* said in bond-space. "Go! Before the crowd regroups. North, to the gate! I will guide you."

She needed no other urging. Kicking the starter, she leaned; the cycle slewed around, and she was running—flying—the crowd momentarily shouting behind her—and then lost in the roar of the wind in her ears.

#

"Theo, I apologize," *Bechimo* said. "I—you took harm from that fall; the shielding I could deploy along such a distance . . ."

Theo, crouched low over the handlebars, most of her concentration on traffic, managed, "What?"

"You called for shielding, but—"

She blinked, realized that she wasn't crete-burned, though her ribs were hurting her again.

"You shielded me?" she asked. "How?"

"The captain and the ship are bonded," he began, and she interrupted him as she accelerated around a taxi.

"Right. But I didn't realize you could do anything like that." She leaned, swooped past a slow-moving lorry, and straightened.

"I ought to have done more," *Bechimo* said. "We *are* bonded."

"It was too far, and I didn't give you any warning," she said. "We need to practice, that's all. I took a lot less harm than I would have, if you hadn't gotten me *some* shielding."

"Turn right at the corner upcoming," *Bechimo* said, and Theo leaned hard, scaring a couple crossing the street into a mad leap for the sidewalk. She wished she knew what Val Con had done to make the machine roar a warning.

"What," she asked, "did I input into this cycle's keypad?"

"The emergency start-up code. Joyita passed it to me; I passed it to you."

"Oh. Well—good work. Where am I going?"

"Jeeves points out that with the unrest in the city, one woman alone on a duocycle would be better served by taking cover soonest, rather than attempting to come out the Port Road to—to her ship. You are therefore being routed to Lady Kareen's house, which is well-defended. You will be safe there until the situation on the streets has been resolved."

"Good thinking," Theo said. "How far?"

"Three blocks, straight on. You will enter by the kitchen door. Staff is expecting you. Lady Kareen and your mother will be apprised of your arrival, once you are safe inside."

"OK then; guide me in."

* * *

"Miri," Jeeves said. "Emissary Twelve has broken contact with the Tree. She appears somewhat disoriented. Pilot yos'Phelium is approaching her with caution; Pilot tey'Doshi is standing back-up."

"Right."

A nice walk in the garden would do her good, she thought wryly, pushing back from the desk.

"Let Pilot tey'Doshi know that I'm on my way, in case Emissary Twelve starts in on the same note she left off on."

"Yes, Miri."

She left the office and headed for the nearest garden-side door, stopping to take a sweater off the hook and pull it on before going outside. The Tree kept the garden warm for the Surebleak season, but nothing like Liad-warm.

"Everything peaceful?" she asked Jeeves as she swung onto the path.

"Emissary Twelve remains subdued. Pilot yos'Phelium has inquired if she is in distress."

That, Miri thought, didn't sound—exactly comforting. She'd rather not return the Elders' errand-Turtle to them with an impairment. On the other hand, who knew what the Tree—

#

A loud roar shattered her thoughts. The path, the garden, and the house vanished into a dizzying sweep of 'crete passing 'way too close to the end of her nose—and receding, her view now of a port street and, straight ahead, pedestrians jumping out of the way.

She was, she realized inside Val Con's head, looking out of his eyes. There was the sense of someone at her back, which she hoped was Theo, and a general feeling of flying.

Val Con leaned, sharp; the duocycle shot into an alley and straightened, hurtling down the very center of the way, the walls on either side bare inches from the end of the handlebars.

Ahead, Miri could see the end of the alley, and too many people milling around beyond it.

"Jeeves?" Val Con asked.

"Flash-crowd," Jeeves said. "I advise you not to slow down."

Val Con crouched low over the bars, kicked the accelerator, thumbed a lever hard, and suddenly they were roaring.

Roaring, they leapt, briefly airborne, out of the alley's mouth, straight into the crowd.

People shouted; people scattered; a couple sleet-for-brains jumped in front of them, but Val Con kept the 'cycle steady, and they leapt away at the last minute.

Something came rolling out of the crowd—a long cylinder maybe made of wood. It hit the front wheel, the 'cycle wobbled—and came upright, steady, speed undiminished.

Miri took a breath—and here was another roller, angling for the back wheel—

"Jump!" Val Con yelled, and Miri saw Theo hit and roll out of the side of her eye, and then there wasn't time for anything else, because the 'cycle bucked, screamed—Val Con was leaping into a somersault the instant before it went down, sliding across the 'crete, still screaming.

They rolled, came to their feet, and staggered as a rock slammed into their shoulder.

The crowd was all around them, yelling and moving fast. More rocks became airborne; one guy reached out to grab them, but they somersaulted away, hitting the ground and rolling, tucked, arms over their head, while the shouting grew louder.

Never aspired to die in a riot, she said then.

Good, he answered.

Through the crowd's noise, she heard a duocycle roar—more than one, maybe—getting louder, faster. The yelling turned to screaming, and boots thudding, the oppression of gathered bodies vanished, and they came up onto their heels, crouching, turning, as one 'cycle flew by, its roar deafening, chasing the crowd away from them—and here came the second, slowing a fraction as the driver held his arm down.

They grabbed him above the elbow—and swung astride.

Their rescuer kicked the accelerator, roaring as they raced after the first, and they saw Theo up on a 'cycle, ahead of them, heading for the North Gate, and it looked like they were going to catch her, but the leader swung wide, heading south inside the port, their 'cycle following, and Miri felt a little nudge of concern, but, no, it made sense to split up, and give whoever might be following two targets to worry about.

In fact, Miri thought, she wouldn't be surprised if the leader peeled off, too, at the next likely-looking exit.

Except, that's not what happened. Both 'cycles made another swooping loop, and hit the accelerators again, drivers leaning near flat across the bars, and them curled low behind theirs. They managed to get a peek sideways, and the nudge of concern became a flicker of actual fear.

They weren't heading out of the port; and they weren't heading for any of the several safe-places inside the port. They were heading for the hotpads.

Miri felt her stomach flutter.

Now, she said. *It's gonna be now.*

Soonest begun, soonest done, Val Con answered. *Cha'trez, you should leave me now.*

She ignored that, instead focusing ahead.

Likely looking jumping off point ahead at one o'clock.

I see it.

The 'cycle they were on wasn't wasting any time. They had hardly identified the dismount point before they were upon it, and Val Con leaping from the back, somersaulting behind the confusion of hoses and repair lines tangled around the single-ship to the right.

They came up into a crouch, and began working their way to the other side of the ship, where they crouched again, concealed by the shadow of its gantry, ears and eyes straining.

The regular and normal sounds of a hot-pad yard came to them, which didn't, Miri thought, mean much, given how quiet duocycles ran when they weren't intentionally making noise.

Val Con was calculating; she could *feel* it, like an itch inside her skull. Too bad she didn't have access to what he was measuring, on the other hand, she'd played this game before, herself.

It was best to stay under cover as much as possible. Unfortunately, while there were plenty of *things* in the area, not many of them provided good cover. The spaces between the ships had to be negotiated, and once they were discovered, they'd be easy targets.

"Jeeves," Val Con murmured. "Can we get surveillance?"

"*Bechimo* has found both duocycles standing at the place where you left their party. He sees other 'cycles in the area, but there seems no way to discover their affiliation. The two pilots who rescued you are both Scouts. Joyita pulled their IDs and I confirm."

"Scouts heading for a hot-pad," Val Con murmured; "not Scout Headquarters."

"We theorize that these are Liaden Scouts," Jeeves said, "who may wish to return you to Headquarters, for discipline."

Miri felt him reject that, though he didn't bother to argue with Jeeves. Instead, he leaned out from their cover a little, frowning down the row of ships.

"How near are the other 'cycles?" he asked.

"Two avenues to the east."

"Location of nearest safe, or defensible, location?"

Jeeves hesitated.

"You are on the opposite side of the port from nearly all of our allies and safeplaces. The yard repair barn is nearby and possibly defensible. If you remain where you are, I will send a car."

"No," Val Con said sharply. "I want no one else in this."

"Understood."

"*Bechimo* allows me to know that he has acquired the two targets—by which he means the duocycles opposite your location. He tells me that he can neutralize them."

"I'm touched," Val Con murmured. "Please ask *Bechimo* to hold fire. What is Theo's situation?"

"En route to Lady Kareen; she has not been pursued."

"Excellent. Where is the repair barn?"

"To your left, at the end of this row—two avenues distant."

"Staff?"

"One person in the back office."

Val Con nodded.

"That will be my target."

Get Liz to mobilize some mercs for an extraction, Miri said.

She felt him not like that, and added.

'less you're set on living in the repair barn, or have hard facts about those Scouts?

A very slight hesitation, before he said, *They may be Scouts, though the odds do not favor that interpretation. Best to have the mercs.*

"Jeeves, ask Commander Lizardi to move armed backup to the repair barn. Position report, please."

"Contacting Commander Lizardi. The duocycles that had been loitering two avenues to the east have moved on. The duocycles which brought you here are still parked opposite your position."

"Any sign of the drivers?"

"No, sir."

Worse and worse, he said, possibly to himself, and she felt him gather himself for the sprint down to the repair barn.

Now, he said, and they were gone, running at his top speed, keeping to shadow, weaving under gantries, and around bucket lifts. Miri ran with him, keeping both eyes open and ears stretched wide.

A shadow moved under the gantry ahead.

Val Con dodged left, ducked under the belly of the ship across the avenue, and kept on going. Nobody came after them.

Nobody had to, after all; they were waiting in the repair barn.

The first swung out to meet them; Val Con spun—there was a cough, very polite in its way, and the pellet hit him in the thigh.

He went down, rolling to come up on his elbows—and froze, looking up into the barrel of the—dart gun.

Horror lifted Miri out of his head, but not before she heard the gunman say, in the mode of Comrade.

"Well met, Agent yos'Phelium. Commander of Agents has called you in for debriefing."

Chapter Eleven

Surebleak

Dudley Avenue and Farley Lane

Theo pushed the duocycle under the back steps, then went up those same steps, slowly, feeling a little gone in the knees.

"Been a full day," she muttered, and raised a hand to knock on the on the door.

It opened before her knuckles connected, and the door guard she'd met when she'd come down to see Kamele—Dilly?—waved her in to a small room with jackets hanging on hooks, and boots set under a built in bench.

"Where'd you leave the 'cycle?" she asked, locking the door behind them.

"I put it under the steps. Figured it would be best if it was out of sight, even a little."

"Good," Dilly said, "Pary'll bring it inside." She paused, giving Theo a critical once-over.

"Let's get you in to Esil. I'll let the professor and the Lady know you're here safe. They're both in the middle, so's you got time for a cuppa somethin' warm and a bite. Right in here."

She leaned past Theo, and opened another door, pushing it wide.

"You go on, now. Nothin's happened up this far, but we ain't slidin' on chance. Got the doors and windows spotted, and Gert's up on the roof, keepin' an eye out."

"Thank you," Theo said.

Dilly shook her head.

"You think we're not gonna open for the professor's own daughter and the Lady's niece? Go on in the kitchen, get something warm inside you, relax. We got your back."

Feeling that something more was required, yet not willing to risk another thank you, Theo inclined her head, and went through the door, into the kitchen.

"There you are, now!" said the plump person at the stove. "You sit on down at the snack table, there, and warm yourself up. You want coffee or tea? Got both."

"Tea, please," Theo said, finding a small, scarred table pushed against the wall near the stove, and slipping into the chair that gave her the best view of Esil, the stove, and the rest of the kitchen.

Her fingers hurt, she noticed; and her face. She suddenly realized that she was *cold*.

"Tea, coming right up. Got some cheese biscuits left over from lunch steaming back up t'warm; they'll be over in a minute. You'll tell me you want soup, sammich, or anything else."

"Just tea's fine, thanks."

Esil put the mug on the table, and stood looking down at her, hands on ample hips.

"Din't I hear you was beat up in a fight this mornin', afore spending the late afternoon ridin' a cycle all over t'city and port, while you got no jacket on, an' no gloves, neither?"

There wasn't, Theo thought, any point arguing with the truth, though it was interesting that Esil was so well-informed.

"It's been a busy day," she admitted. "Cheese rolls would be good, thanks." Her stomach growled suddenly, and she sighed, looking up into the cook's knowing face.

"And maybe a bowl of soup, too."

"That's the way it's done," Esil said approvingly. "You eat somethin', warm yourself up. Get a bath, put on some clothes don't look like they been dragged down the street, an' you'll be fine."

She turned back to the stove. Theo picked up the mug and had a cautious taste.

The last cup of tea she'd had in Lady Kareen's house had been Joyful Sunrise, a citrus-mint breakfast tea. This was darker, smoky, with an unexpectedly sweet undernote. It was better than Bitter Truth, though that, thought Theo, could be said of most tea, and, once she had gotten used to the sweet note, good on its own terms.

She sighed, and sipped again. Her eyes started to close—and came open at the sound of a small click, which was Esil putting a plate of cheese rolls down in front of her.

"Soup's coming," she said. "You get started on them."

"Thank you," said Theo, picking up a roll and breaking it open. It smelled delicious, and tasted better.

"*Bechimo*," she said in bond-space; "please let Exec O'Berin know that I've reached a position of safety."

"Yes, Theo."

"Also," she said, breaking open another roll; "the crew can stand down, unless there is an on-going situation that I'm not aware of."

"Yes," *Bechimo* said again. "Please, eat and rest. Your biologic systems are in disarray. You must not risk yourself."

She managed not to laugh outloud, which was good, because here was Esil coming back with a bowl of soup.

"Thanks," she said, and received a pat on the shoulder as the cook turned to the stove.

"You eat up. When you're done, I'll take you upstairs, so's you can have a nice hot shower. They found some clean clothes oughta fit you fine, and a coat."

Esil turned around to shake a finger at Theo.

"What was you thinkin', going outside on a day like this with no coat?"

"I had a jacket," Theo told her. "It was stolen."

Esil sniffed.

"Some people's children," she said, darkly, and moved back to the stove.

* * *

"Jeeves!" Miri shouted. "Where are those mercs?"

"On the way; they will not arrive in time to prevent Master Val Con from being taken aboard *Seilaht*, out of Solcintra, Liad."

"Can you disable the ship?"

"Yes. *Bechimo* tells me that he can make the shot, but the damage will be . . . extreme."

"Not acceptable."

Miri extended her mental fingers—but he was gone, not present; the him of him a hazy pattern seen through a snow squall—which would be the effects of the dart-delivered drug.

"Track *Seilaht*; don't let it out of your sight," she snapped, turning back toward the house. "Mr. Joyita likes to pry into people's secrets—tell him to get me the Jump coords, the Struven signature, anything at all that we can trace."

"Yes."

"Miri!"

She looked over her shoulder, though she didn't stop. Daav and Aelliana weren't quite running full out, and Emissary Twelve effortlessly keeping up.

"Good," she said. "All of you, come with me."

"Jeeves reports Val Con has been acquired by the Department of the Interior," Aelliana said, from her right side.

"I'm going after him, now," Miri answered.

"Korval--" Daav began from her left side--and she shook her head, once, violently, cutting him off.

"*Van'chela*, you recently solved for this exact equation," Aelliana said. "Have you forgotten already? *If one is taken, both are compromised.* Of course, she must go. Not only to mount a rescue, if it can be done, but to shield the clan."

"Agreed," Daav said. "Miri, who is your pilot?"

"I am," said Emissary Twelve.

Miri stumbled, stopped, and turned to face her.

"You?" she asked. "I thought you have orders from the Elders."

"A dragon of the Great Tree has been stolen from his duty," Emissary Twelve said sharply. "His recovery must be my first priority."

Miri looked at Daav, who looked at Aelliana, who looked at Miri.

"How're you going to follow a Jump-ship?" she asked. "I assume yours uses the same drive as the big rocks."

"My ship is more subtle than the larger vessels," Emissary Twelve said. "I can follow; and I will not lose them. I will need coordinates and identifiers; and my board."

Miri blinked at her.

"Go, then, and get set up--Jeeves, patch in Mr. Joyita and *Bechimo*, and get Emissary Twelve what she needs."

"Yes, Miri."

Emissary Twelve inclined slightly from the waist, more-or-less, and hurried away in the direction of the driveway and her ship. Miri spun on a heel and trotted toward the house.

"I can pilot myself," she said. "By the way."

"Can you, if Val Con is . . . unavailable?" Daav asked.

"Good question. I been taking lessons, but we don't know what'll happen, if one of us leaves the loop permanently. Not really any good way to do a pretest."

"No," Daav said softly; "there isn't."

They were approaching the side door, which opened as they approached.

"Jeeves," Miri said; "I want Kareen, full screen, in the morning parlor. Delm's Emergency, tell her."

"Yes, Miri."

"You will need clothes," Aelliana said; "your jacket. Give me leave to pack for you."

Miri nodded, and Aelliana peeled off, running lightly down the hall to the back stairs.

"Jeeves, let Aelliana into our room."

"Done."

Miri swept into the morning parlor, and stood before the screen, legs braced. She felt Daav come to rest behind her left shoulder, covering her off-side, and her stomach cramped, feeling that last sweep of horror from Val Con all over again—

The screen flickered, and Kareen was with her, sharp eyes moving from her face to Daav's and back.

"Korval." She bowed, full respect to the delm.

"Yes," Miri said, delm to clan member. "There is an emergency. You will listen; you will not interrupt; you will acknowledge that you have understood me; and you will obey. Am I clear?"

"Korval, you are."

"The delm has been compromised, and the Ring has fallen into the hands of the clan's enemies. Until such time as this situation has been repaired, you will hold Korval in trust for the *na'delm*, Talizea yos'Phelium.

"Jeeves will open all records to you. He will provide Ms. dea'Gauss with a record of this meeting, so that she may do everything that is needful, for the good of the clan.

"Your first task will naturally be to publicly inform the Council of Bosses that, pursuant to Paragraph Seven, Clause Nine, the Road Boss, Val Con yos'Phelium and Miri Robertson, have sub-let the position to Kor Vid yos'Phelium and Daaneka tey'Doshi. They will provide a resume; Professor Waitley will test them for administrative aptitude. These documents will be made available to the Bosses."

She paused to review, figured she'd hit the highlights, and Kareen'd do the needful--no sense starting in to micromanage, even if she had time.

"Do you understand what I have said?" she asked.

It might have been an artifact of the screen, or the lighting in whatever room Kareen happened to be in, down there in the city, but it seemed like she'd paled somewhat, and for a long moment Miri thought she wasn't going to answer.

Then, Kareen bowed, a potent weave of I am not Worthy, and Honor to the Delm.

"Korval, I hear, I understand, and I will obey," she said, the High Tongue ringing like so many icy bells.

Miri took a breath.

"Excellent," she said. "The Ring, the clan, and its treasures, passes, in trust, to Kareen yos'Phelium. It is done."

She bowed, low, clan member to delm, and heard Daav take a careful breath, before he, too, bowed.

"*Korval-pernard'i*," he murmured.

Kareen looked at him over Miri's shoulder, and inclined her head.

"Kor Vid yos'Phelium, I See you," she murmured.

She then spread her hands, showing empty palms, and spoke to Miri.

"I release you to your task, which is of utmost importance to the clan. Solve it quickly, Pilot, and return to us."

"Korval," Miri said, and turned to the door.

The last thing she heard before she stepped into the hallway was Kareen saying, "Jeeves, please send the recording of this meeting to all adult clan members, and to Ms. dea'Gauss."

Aelliana met her in the hall, passing over a travel-bag and a leather jacket.

"We will take good care of Talizea, Miri," she said softly, and Miri swallowed, feeling that like a strike to the heart. Gods, gods, Lizzie. And neither of them likely to get out of this alive . . .

"Thank you," she said to Aelliana, and took a hard breath. "It would be good if Kamele could come spend some time with her, too."

"Of course," Aelliana said. "Go, now—fetch your lifemate, and come home to us quickly."

There wasn't anything to say to that. Aelliana knew to the last decimal point just how likely it was that Miri could fetch Val Con home again. Wordless, she bowed, turned and ran down the hall, scarcely paying attention to how she went. The door before her opened, and she rushed out—

Into the garden.

She ran down the overgrown path, to the Tree Court; to the Tree itself. Dropping the bag, she shrugged into her jacket, squinting up into the high branches.

"I don't have a lotta time," she said.

A breeze kissed her cheek, bearing the suggestion that the situation was perhaps not quite dire.

"Easy for you to say;" Miri said bitterly; "you still got dragons, and you'll get more if we die out."

The air conveyed the idea that the Tree understood that she was upset, but that she was mistaken if she thought that the Tree failed to properly appreciate each of its dragons. The quality of thought turned slightly acerbic: If they were each and all the same, the Tree would have an easier time keeping up with them. But, no, they were all individuals, to be tended individually – and the Tree valued each.

Remembered each.

Miri took a breath – and extended a hand before she realized that she was hearing a pod, descending through the leaves.

She'd barely caught it before it fell open in her palm, and had eaten it before she realized that it had no odor at all.

More racket came from the high branches, and she held out her hands, catching one . . . three . . . five . . . seven pods of differing sizes. Quickly, she stowed them in the pockets of her jacket, and raised her hands to catch the rest.

The last of the pods pocketed, the breeze abruptly turned sharp, pushing at her, insistent. She grabbed the bag, slung it over a shoulder and ran back the way she had come.

Emissary Twelve met her at the rock, which was cold as the air, now, and showing reflective surfaces. She took the bag, and passed through the hatch into the ship, Miri following.

Inside was weirdly familiar; a very small scale replica of the bridge of Edger's ship, that she and Val Con had used—well, it wasn't all that long ago, not by the count of years, anyway.

Emissary Twelve turned from lashing Miri's bag into a cubby cut into the rock wall.

"You will sit there," she said, pointing with one three-fingered hand.

Miri sank on the rocky ledge indicated, and looked straight ahead, into the view-tank.

"I have several signatures from this ship that has captured the Tree's dragon," Emissary Twelve said, sitting on the ledge directly before the tank, and a panel of instruments.

"How are you going to be able to track them?" Miri asked. "Not only is a Jump ship, but it's probably a Scout ship—really fast, and really slippery."

Emissary Twelve made a sound that could have been a sigh, or a laugh.

"None of that matters; the ship may fly away from us with all speed, yet, we will always come to rest beside her. I have entangled this vessel's signatures with theirs. In the eyes of the universe, we are one."

Well, thought Miri, that explained everything nice and tidy, didn't it?

There came a quiet hiss, and Miri turned to see the hatch coming down. There was no seam where it joined the rest of the rock; no seals; nothing to show that there was, or had ever been, a hatch there.

"They lift," Emissary Twelve said, her fingers moving deliberately among her instruments.

She pressed the crystal button set in the center of her board.

"We follow."

* * *

The door closed behind Esil, and Theo heaved a sigh of relief.

Food, and tea, and the ambiance of the kitchen had warmed her, so she thought she might not need a shower—an opinion she rapidly changed when she caught sight of herself in a hallway mirror.

Her hair was a knotted snarl hanging over one ear; her face showing bruises where Jake had hit her; her sweater—what was left of it between the holes—was liberally streaked with mud, and grease.

Her pants were scarred and muddy, but at least they hadn't torn, and her boots were going to need serious attention. Aside from all of that, she was grubby, and one look at the green sweater and flowing black pants that had been laid out for her, made up her mind.

She pulled her sweater over her head, hissing when her ribs complained, and dropped it to the floor. Sitting down on the stool, she tugged off her boots, and her socks, stood up to pull her belt off, and skin out of her pants, which dropped to the floor with a definite *thud*.

Theo frowned—then shook her head.

"Right," she said aloud, "Val Con's small weapon."

She found the leg pocket and reached inside to pull out the pouch she'd taken out of her brother's jacket. Now that she wasn't distracted by trying not to fall off the back of a racing duocycle, it felt heavier than she expected for a small weapon, and in fact, seem to be two things, not one.

Walking over the to the table where her clean clothes had been laid out, she upended the pouch.

A flat, dull black metal rectangle fell onto the green sweater – Theo shook her head as she recognized a flat-fold knife. In its current, folded flat state, it was perfectly safe. Trip the corner safety, though, and you were suddenly holding a three-inch, *very* sharp cutting edge, which was undoubtedly dangerous, but mostly to the person using it.

Still, it was a weapon, and she would have absolutely used it, say, on Jake, if she'd had the chance.

Something glimmered against the sweater, drawing her eye. She leaned closer, and after a moment located the source. A ring. In fact, a rather large ring, which had landed on its face, leaving the broad band to catch the light from the overhead fixture.

Theo extended a finger and turned it over.

"Pharst!"

Korval's Tree-and-Dragon shone in bright enamel work, the clan's motto, *Flaran Cha'menthi*—I Dare—framed by two large emeralds—one showing a dark crack at its heart, the other tinged with yellow.

She had seen this ring just this morning.

On Val Con's hand.

She shivered.

"Theo?" *Bechimo* asked in bond-space. "Are you ill?"

"Something bad just happened," she said, taking a deep breath, and moving her eyes from the Ring. "I don't understand it, but—where's Val Con?"

There was a small pause before *Bechimo* answered.

"Your brother has been captured by enemies of his clan. Miri has gone in pursuit after making Lady Kareen *Korval-pernard'i*."

The meaning of that last came through as *Korval-in-Trust*.

Theo closed her eyes.

"Lady Kareen is safe?"

"Indeed. She is in her parlor, accessing such files as are of immediate necessity to Korval. Jeeves has reinforced extended his protections over the house."

"All right," said Theo. Either Lady Kareen knew Val Con had given her the Ring to deliver, or she didn't. In either case, there was time to take a shower.

So she could show a clean face to the delm.

* * *

The recording ended with his mother—with *Korval-pernard'i*—directing Jeeves to distribute it to all adult clan members. Pat Rin closed his eyes, and reviewed a mental exercise to steady the nerves, and sharpen the wits. It was a pilot's exercise, Pat Rin having grown up in a clan where very nearly all his kin were pilots, though he had come late to the duty. Instead, he had used this particular exercise for most of his life as an aid to gambling and card-play, the activities which had funded himself and his household.

He might, of course, have claimed his quartershare, but pride—he supposed it must have been pride, if it were simply not arrant stupidity—had him spurn the clan's money, as he was no pilot, and therefore no use to the clan.

The door to his office opened.

"Pat Rin—what has happened?"

He opened his eyes, and met his lifemate's depthless black eyes.

"Val Con—" he began, but his voice choked out. He shook his head, and took a drink of cold tea from the cup on desk to clear his throat.

"Val Con has been abducted by a pair of what Jeeves believes to be agents of the DOI."

Her face shuttered.

"Is it known where he is being held?"

Pat Rin waved a hand at the screen.

"Auxiliary information is apparently being compiled. What we have at the moment is a recording of Korval Herself making Kareen yos'Phelium *Korval-pernard'i.*"

"In trust," Natesa said, momentarily puzzled—her eyes widening as she understood.

"In trust *for Lizzie?*"

"Yes," he said, extending a hand. "Precisely for Lizzie."

Natesa stepped forward and took his hand, looking down into his face, her own troubled.

"Miri has gone after Val Con?"

"As she must. They are linked; she is an open door to Korval, if Val Con . . ."

His voice faded, but he scarcely needed to finish that sentence for Juntavas Judge Natesa the Assassin.

His desk unit chimed—message incoming.

"Possibly, this is the answer to all our questions," he murmured, leaning forward to tap the screen.

Natesa sat on the arm of his chair, slipping her arm around his shoulders, pressing companionably against his side.

The file was encrypted; Korval house code. Pat Rin entered his key, and information bloomed on the screen.

"We have confirmation: the abductors are agents of the Department of the Interior," he said, around a sudden feeling of queasiness.

"Yes, certainly," Natesa murmured, leaning to the screen and scrolling gently through the information displayed there.

"I think I see," she said, after she had reached the end of the file.

"What do you see?" Pat Rin wondered.

"I see that Captain Lisle was hired to take up the Road Boss—Val Con *or* Miri will accomplish the DOI's purpose for them. She and her compatriots watch the office, and—in a burst of luck, Theo visits her brother there. Captain Lisle may or may not believe that she has both Road Bosses, but she clearly thinks that the chance provided to take both is worth her risk. Perhaps it is; she does take Theo, though it is an expensive acquisition for her."

"Theo is not Miri," Pat Rin protested.

Natesa shrugged.

"That is immaterial. Ultimately, the agents of the DOI want Val Con or Miri, but Theo has high value as bait. Val Con will scarcely leave his sister in the hands of pirates, especially after it is demonstrated that she was helpless to prevent them taking her jacket from her. When Jeeves calls for duocyclists to assist in the rescue attempt, how easy for a pair—or more—of the agents we know to be on the planet to join the host. Theo, having served her purpose, is allowed to escape; Val Con is acquired."

She looked down into his eyes.

"The DOI wants Korval; they need only one half of a true lifemating to achieve this. Break one; command both."

Pat Rin's stomach cramped. He took a hard breath and reached to the screen, scrolling once more through the information—and pausing at a notation.

"I think," he said, his eyes on the screen, "that we now know who has been tutoring Boss Surebleak, and who is funding the Take Backers."

"Yes," said Natesa; "I think we do, too."

* * *

Her last voyage via Clutch ship had been on Edger's vessel, docked at Prime Station around a planet called Lufkit. Then, the pressing of the crystal knob at the center of the board had immediately made the stars go away. At the time, Miri had thought that meant Clutch ships moved really fast.

She'd soon learned that the opposite was true. Clutch ships weren't slow, but were . . . limited by the peculiarities of the Electron Substitution Drive, which required a dense field to operate. So, instead of what sane ships did in terms of seeking Jump points and doing their level best to avoid dense systems and starfields that would interfere with the utilization of their drives–Clutch ships sought out gravity wells and cluttered star systems, using the curious habit of electrons to appear elsewhere before they left their original orbit as a means of motion, if not propulsion. It wasn't ordinary star flight by human standards, but it did the job.

Eventually.

The other thing that made Clutch ships sort of stand out was that they tested the space away from their starting position before they committed to leaving that position and fully occupying the new one. Miri had never seen a vid of a Clutch ship traveling through space, which she figured was just fine.

Emissary Twelve's little boulder, now . . .

It slammed into the air like it was using the mass of Surebleak entire to thrust against—which it probably was.

Miri, thrown back hard into her stone chair, bit her tongue, eyes tearing, and ears popping. Her head hit the wall, and she saw stars, though not the local ones.

When her sight cleared, she saw Jelaza Kazone, the Tree, in the bottom third of the view-tank, and in the upper third, the depths of space.

Speaking with back straight and attention on the screens, Emissary Twelve might have been talking for her own benefit, except she spoke in Liaden.

"Here I measure the local constants so I might instruct the ship itself to return here with you, if need be, without my presence. Also, I confirm and reaffirm the constants reported to me by the *T'carais* of the Knife Clan, known to you as Edger. The ship also tells me of this system's distant cloud of dust wishing to become a gas planet, which we will use rather than this star for our next transition. My extreme attention will be required when we arrive at that cloud; I may be required to act rapidly in order to take best advantage. It would be best if you remain quiet until next I speak with you. Also, cushion yourself, for our entanglement requires motion."

In the view tank Miri made out part of the port road, the slight widening where the Road Boss shared the road's width with their neighbor, and the canopy of the tree itself. She thought she saw a car rushing up the road – and heard Emissary Twelve began to hum, to sing!

And then the view tank's image meant nothing, her sight reft from her by the pressure of back against stone as electrons danced to the tune called by the young Clutch turtle.

* * *

The delm had made plans.

Kareen yos'Phelium leaned back in her chair and closed her eyes.

Of course the delm had made plans. It was the business of delms to make plans, after all, and Korval delms moreso than many.

Most especially *this* Korval delm, who had taken up the Ring as Korval's salvation . . .

. . . and its doom.

That the Ring now came to her to hold in trust for the True Heir—that was not only just, it was so flagrantly necessary that one could only bow and do all that was required.

One might pause for a moment, now, having closed one file, and before opening the next, to reflect upon her anger, so many years ago, when her delm had offered her this same duty—take the Ring, and keep Korval safe, for the *na'delm.*

Ah, how one had frozen the face – just so! And how one had refused anything less than her ascension to *Korval Herself,* who would steer the clan away from the cliffs that had threatened them, seen their numbers increased, their alliances multiplied, and their social standing cemented. Oh, she had been terrible in her disdain.

And she had been so very certain.

Oh, my, yes, but she had been—not young, certainly, not by that point – though a case could be made for both naive and arrogant.

Had she also been wrong?

Well – perhaps she had; perhaps she had not.

Many things, after all, would have remained the same.

Daav would still have removed himself from the clan; Val Con would still have grown up and enlisted in the Scouts, as the children of yos'Phelium so very often did. Likely, this Department of the Interior would have recruited him just the same; a Scout Commander is surely a prize worth winning – and the Department had long since included Korval among its inventory of those to be eradicated.

So, perhaps nothing would have changed very much . . .

And now, she was *Korval-pernard'i*, trusted to hold the Ring, and the clan, safe, for the *na'delm*.

And, therefore, to duty.

She opened her eyes, leaned toward the computer and glanced up at a small sound that had emanated from the door of her study. Possibly, she thought, it had been meant as a knock. She ought at least to test the theory; a delm of Korval would do no less.

"Come!" she called.

The door opened sufficient to admit the lanky form of her niece, Theo, looking rather paler than usual, her hair pulled back with an unaccustomed severity that only served to cast the bruises adorning her face into high relief.

Her eyes were wide, and very dark, and for a moment Kareen thought she was looking at an incidence of deep shock. However, after a moment to gather herself, Theo produced a very credible bow in the mode of younger to elder, which was perfectly unexceptional from niece to aunt.

"*Bechimo* says that you're delm-in-trust," she said, in Terran, which, Kareen thought, spoke eloquently of the state of her mind. It was a point of pride, with Theo, to address her in Liaden.

In *proper* Liaden.

Kareen inclined her head.

"*Bechimo's* information is accurate," she said, also in Terran. "A sudden reversal in my estate."

Give the child credit, she caught the irony; pale lips bent in a wan smile even as she stepped to the desk, and held out her hand, so that Kareen could see the object resting on her palm.

She raised her eyebrows, and looked up into Theo's face.

"How very—unexpected. We had thought the Ring taken."

"Val Con," Theo said. "He—when he picked me up out of—he said there was a small weapon in his pocket, and I should take it. I didn't—I didn't need it, forgot I had it until just now, when I was getting ready to shower."

"Quite. I might myself allow it to be somewhat larger than a *small* weapon, but he would know best how to value it."

Theo shook her head slightly.

"There was a flat-fold, too."

"Excellent," Kareen murmured, and forced herself to extend a hand, and take Korval's Ring into her possession.

"I thought he was safe," Theo said, then, dropping back a few steps. "If I'd known he was still in trouble, I would've gone after him; I wouldn't have let him –"

Kareen raised her hand, stemming the flow.

"Certainly, he knew this," she said gently. "We do not abandon our kin to danger. However, it is obvious that he understood the situation, and the manner of danger which pursued him. Knowing these things, he acted to keep the Ring safe. This is no trivial task he entrusted to you, Niece."

She held the Ring up between forefinger and thumb.

"You have, in a sense that goes beyond mere delms, preserved the integrity of the clan."

The black eyes glittered. Theo blinked and glanced away for a moment, as if she were Liaden-born and distressed by this public display of emotion.

"*Bechimo* also says that—he's been taken by enemies of the clan, and that Miri's gone after."

"This is also so. I hold the Ring in trust for Talizea, the *na'delm*."

Theo took a hard breath.

"I can go after them," she said. "Miri'll need back-up."

Ah, this was delicate, Kareen thought; and there was Korval pride to placate, as well.

"In fact, we do not know that Miri will need back-up," she said gently, putting her hand on the screen before her. "I am reviewing files now, and, while it is plain that there had been a plan, the plan itself is not elucidated. Which is wise.

"I do not hide from you the fact that this event has left us very thin, indeed, and I hope that you will not find it presumptuous in me to ask, as your aunt, if you will not stay with us, until we can gather ourselves together, call in allies, or hire them."

She tipped her head, and smiled.

"I would take it kindly, again, as your aunt, if you might assist us in this way."

Theo considered her so long that Kareen feared she had lost her subtlety.

Then, the girl bowed—younger to elder, once more.

"Val Con and I talked . . . a little before we got . . . interrupted. He was explaining how Korval was going to be shifting focus, from clan to kin," she said, haltingly.

"Indeed," Kareen said; "I am only just now acquainting myself with this proposal."

Theo nodded.

"In any case, yes. I will stay, and do what I can to help the family."

Author's Afterword

So . . . wow, right?

You really can't deny that *The Wrong Lance* got on its bike and *rode*.

Interestingly, some folks found the pace–which is similar to that of *Agent of Change*, the little novel that started it all, and which other readers profess to prefer, finding latter Liaden books "too slow" and even "boring"–too quick and even "breathless."

Which just goes to show that you can't please everyone, so you might as well please yourself.

And that brings us back to the vexed question of why *The Wrong Lance* staggered and died. It *should* have been fun. In fact it *was* fun, right up until it died, on the up-note of Theo's promise–and refused to go on.

So what *did* go wrong?

Well. First, as I mentioned in my introductory notes, was that I started in the wrong place. It is Traditional, when writing sequels, to start the next book where the previous book left off. Pretty often, we here in the Liaden Universe® avoid this by starting the next book with a new character/problem that may or may not intersect the previous book at some point, or merely run in parallel.

Unfortunately, this time, I was stuck with doing a direct sequel and no way I could worm my way out of it, so–knowing even then that it was a misstep, but thinking that I could make a recover–I started the new book where the previous book had left off.

The arrival of the Clutch short life, Emissary Twelve, front and center right at the very beginning of the story, is a signal–to readers and to the story brain–that Emissary Twelve, and the problem she bears, will be central to the book and its resolution. Emissary Twelve, therefore, had a lot to do with the shape taken by *The Wrong Lance*. She comes demanding to immediately see the Destroyer of the Universe, and it is very strongly hinted that the Clutch Elders are Displeased.

It was remarked by more than one reader of *The Wrong Lance* that Emissary Twelve did not act like a "typical" Clutch person. Early on, one reader asked if part of what had thrown the story sideways, so to speak, was the "excessive" narration about the short-lives, to which the answer was–yes. And no.

Because, in fact, as is explained in that excess of narration, Emissary Twelve is *not* a typical Clutch. She is one of the short-lives, the all-but-nameless, who are born quickly in order to accomplish a specific task–like wiping out an Yxtrang Conquest Corps–and who then die as quickly as they were born. While Emissary Twelve was not quickened for war, she was woken precisely because she lives faster than typical Clutch, and is more adaptable. She is by nature wary, and predisposed to perceive threat; there's no doubt that she's dangerous. You have to win Emissary Twelve's trust, and it's not easy.

A word of explanation here: The short-lives may be new to readers of the Liaden Universe, but Steve and I have known of them, and their specific function, for more than 30 years. If you look close, you'll see mention of their work in *Agent of Change*, the very first Liaden book ever written.

To recap, the arrival of Emissary Twelve, and her general attitude of belligerence, has, in story-speak, *upped the stakes*. Emissary Twelve must be a major figure in the story, and she must be part of the resolution of the story, aka the Thrilling Conclusion.

Now, in action-adventure fiction, upping the stakes isn't usually seen as a Bad Thing, and there were all those people who were finding the most recent Liaden books boring, slow, and confusing. Maybe, I thought–maybe we *owed* those readers a book harking back to our shared roots.

Let me just pause here and reiterate a Rule of Writing, to wit: When you are writing a book, you are writing for the characters, and you are writing for yourself, the author. To consider the feelings, expectations and probable criticisms of the book's future readers will, at the least push you into the land of second guesses. At the most, it will freeze you solid. There is a time and a place to think about a work's potential audience, but that time is not during the composition of the first draft.

So, allowing considerations of future readers to influence my decision-making at this point was an error. One I should have known better than, but I didn't stop there.

I decided that, since we were upping the stakes and all, that Val Con would be re-attached by the DOI. Long-term readers of my commentary about our work will recall that we have, over the course of twenty-three novels *twice* tried to get Val Con re-attached to the DOI and both times had to back-track and rewrite. I *knew* this, but I thought that, surely this time, with a plan in place and Miri at his back – *this time*, Val Con would allow himself–no! He would with malice aforethought *force* his capture and return to Headquarters, where he would proceed to kick Commander of Agents to the curb. There was a Plan this time; *his* Plan; surely there would be no problem.

I might have noticed his hesitation earlier, had it not been for one other thing. Remember what I said above about writing to please yourself? Well–confession time. I wanted–I wanted oh-so-much to get Val Con on a duocycle to perform a Thrilling Rescue. I wanted – I *wanted* the roar of the throttle, the speed, the spectacle of riding with dozens of others in train.

On the face of it, there was nothing wrong with the duocycle rescue; in fact, it made a couple of useful linkages, said some things about loyalty and family values – and reinforces the rescue attempt going on at *Teramondi's* hatch, by Chernak and Stost, which also says some nice things about loyalty. There is nothing wrong with the duocycle scene through Val Con going down, and Theo–after seeing him "rescued" in his turn–turning toward Lady Kareen's place.

It was only after he was "rescued" that Val Con began to...balk. I explained to him again that he had planned for this; that Theo was safe, that Miri had his back. He seemed to settle down a bit, though as I was getting the chapters ready for upload, I noted that the narrative was starting to become labored, and some of the threads were beginning to unravel.

I probably should have taken the hint and stopped writing immediately, but there was still forward momentum. Miri had to produce an orderly transfer of power and be certain that the clan was held safely. Emissary Twelve, who had eaten of the Tree's gifts and was well on her way to becoming one of its dragons, needed to step forward so that she would be in place at the Thrilling Conclusion, which was her right as a character who had appeared in the first chapter. Miri had to collect the pods from the Tree, destined to be another important part of the Thrilling Conclusion.

Theo had to arrive at Kareen. The Ring had to pass, proving that the delm *had planned this*, and that things were going in the right general direction for the successful completion of that plan.

So, there we are, the Ring has passed, the stakes are as high as they've ever been, in the Liaden Universe (as distinct from the Crystal Universe). Val Con has been captured and is being taken to Headquarters, Miri and Emissary Twelve in hot pursuit, while on the new homeworld, Boss Surebleak has arisen to challenge the Boss Conrad and the New Order.

So many balls in the air! So many active characters! So many active threats! Why, anything could happen!

And what happened was, at that precise point–the story died, the characters stopped talking to me; for a brief time I forgot how to write sentences.

I cast my mind into the future, and what I saw was Val Con becoming Commander of Agents, the only one who was possibly qualified to oversee an orderly and humane shutdown of the DOI–and that was not an acceptable outcome. I moved the pieces around in my head; I tried different scenarios; I–well. Long story short, no conclusion, thrilling or otherwise, that came from the set-up we have just finished reading together—felt right to me. Worse, nothing brought the characters back to life.

Which is when I accepted that I had made a major error in storytelling, and that the only thing I could do was to start over, not at the point where the previous book had ended, but earlier than that. This decision slowed the pace of *Accepting the Lance* considerably, got Rys' team back into the narrative, active, instead of a side note (*all agents lost*), brought the Bedel more fully into the story, allowed Theo to shine, brought Emissary Twelve down from Epic Avenger to a more flexible and definitely more benign short-life.

The stakes did rise, though more slowly, and Korval *protected* Surebleak, sealing the bargain made in *I Dare*.

Do I regret having written the scenes that became *The Wrong Lance*? No. I was delighted to write the duocycle rescue—and it still plays pretty well on re-read. I was pleased to see Theo bonding more closely with her ship and her family. As I said at the beginning of this adventure, there are a lot of good bits, and there's not much wrong with the words—it was only the wrong adventure: too dark, too fast, too...ungiving. Part of the point of the Liaden stories, as they've moved forward, is to celebrate humanity, and compromise, and to show that even people who have lost much can, with the goodwill of others, win back to, and exceed, themselves.

Did I lose anything that I regret from *The Wrong Lance*?

Yes, actually. I regret not being able to write Kareen as Korval-in-Trust, protecting the clan and making it safe from its enemies. Kareen would have been one of the scariest, most thorough Korval delms in the history of the clan. She would have been stringent. And she would have been *right*.

And—here ends the tale and the tale of the tale. It was a fun trip.

Thank you all for your patience, your participation, and your support.

Everybody take care.

Sharon Lee

Central Maine

August 17 2020

About the Authors

Maine-based writers Sharon Lee and Steve Miller teamed up in the late 1980s to bring the world the story of Kinzel, an inept wizard with a love of cats, a thirst for justice, and a staff of true power.

Since then, the husband-and-wife team have written dozens of short stories and twenty plus novels, most set in their star-spanning, nationally-bestselling, Liaden Universe®.

Before settling down to the serene and stable life of a science fiction and fantasy writer, Steve was a traveling poet, a rock-band reviewer, reporter, and editor of a string of community newspapers.

Sharon, less adventurous, has been an advertising copywriter, copy editor on night-side news at a small city newspaper, reporter, photographer, and book reviewer.

Both credit their newspaper experiences with teaching them the finer points of collaboration.

Steve and Sharon are jointly the recipients of the E. E. "Doc" Smith Memorial Award for Imaginative Fiction (the Skylark), one of the oldest awards in science fiction. In addition, their work has won the much-coveted Prism Award (*Mouse and Dragon* and *Local Custom*), as well as the Hal Clement Award for Best Young Adult Science Fiction (*Balance of Trade*), and the Year's Best Military and Adventure SF Readers' Choice Award ("Wise Child").

Sharon and Steve passionately believe that reading fiction ought to be fun, and that stories are entertainment.

Steve and Sharon maintain a web presence at korval.com

Novels by Sharon Lee & Steve Miller

The Liaden Universe®

Fledgling

Saltation

Mouse and Dragon

Ghost Ship

Dragon Ship

Necessity's Child

Trade Secret

Dragon in Exile

Alliance of Equals

The Gathering Edge

Neogenesis

Accepting the Lance

Trader's Leap

Omnibus Editions

The Dragon Variation

The Agent Gambit

Korval's Game

The Crystal Variation

Story Collections

A Liaden Universe Constellation: Volume 1

A Liaden Universe Constellation: Volume 2

A Liaden Universe Constellation: Volume 3

A Liaden Universe Constellation: Volume 4

The Fey Duology

Duainfey

Longeye

Gem ser'Edreth

The Tomorrow Log

Novels by Sharon Lee

The Carousel Trilogy
Carousel Tides
Carousel Sun
Carousel Seas
Jennifer Pierce Maine Mysteries
Barnburner
Gunshy

THANK YOU

Thank you for your support of our work.
Sharon Lee and Steve Miller

Made in United States
North Haven, CT
22 November 2023

44415001R00124